Real P

Stories OF OUR TIME

Linda M. Carpentier

Linda M. Carpentier

STORIES OF OUR TIME
Copyright © 2017 by Linda M. Carpentier

Printed in Canada

ISBN: 978-1-4866-1434-9

Word Alive Press
131 Cordite Road, Winnipeg, MB R3W 1S1
www.wordalivepress.ca

Cataloguing in Publication may be obtained through Library and Archives Canada

CONTENTS

1.

RETIREMENT FOR TWO

HELEN MAYNARD LOOKED AROUND THE LIVING ROOM OF her home with satisfaction. It was a comfortable place, tastefully decorated, filled with morning sunlight. Her eyes lingered over the photos of her children and grandchildren—special blessings to her and Don. She smiled with the realization that tomorrow would begin a new season in their lives.

She thought of their youth and marriage, and the precious time they'd spent together, when every day had been a delight. Then the children had arrived, and much of her time had been focussed on their care.

Don was a mature, responsible husband, caring of his wife and children. His involvement in rearing the children matched hers, but the home was her domain. She liked it that way; the definite division of labour was uncomplicated. Fortunately, it suited them both. Don had little taste for cooking or housekeeping. He had done both in his single days, but after he'd married he was glad to let his wife take care of the household responsibilities. His job kept him busy enough.

Helen had chosen to stay home with her children, finding fulfilment in caring for her home and family. To those who questioned her for doing it, she responded that she had plenty of work to do, and didn't want the stress of a job outside the home; besides, they didn't need extra money or a luxurious lifestyle.

Her friends and family knew she was a happy woman who had everything that mattered to her. Well, almost everything. The one thing she and Don both regretted was that they had never really spent enough time with each other. The carefree companionship of their youth had been forced out by the busyness of their responsibilities.

But that was about to change; Don was retiring. Today was his last day at work.

He had worked hard at his job. For many years it had provided him with a lot of satisfaction. However, in the last few years he had grown weary of it.

"I'm tired of responsibility," he'd said one day. "And I'm tired of schedules, deadlines, and quotas. I want to be footloose and fancy free. I want to sit on the front porch for several hours and watch the world go by. Then when we feel like going somewhere or doing something, we can just go and do it. No advance planning. No waiting for the weekend or holidays. Just be spontaneous."

"What if we took a trip somewhere?" Helen had asked with amusement. "We would need to plan ahead for that."

"Well, yes," he had conceded. "We would need to plan for something like that, but for the most part I want life to be unplanned and unscheduled."

With delightful anticipation, they had both looked forward to the future together.

When Don arrived home that afternoon, he entered the door with a wide smile on his face. "Guess what!" he announced. "I'm retired—and I'm going to enjoy every minute of it!"

Helen smiled, too. "Congratulations."

———✦———

After breakfast the next morning, Don went out to the front porch and sat in a comfortable chair. "Isn't it great to be retired," he remarked to no one in particular. He relaxed there all morning.

After lunch, Helen dressed in her old clothes and wide-brimmed hat and went out to weed her large vegetable garden. Gardening had always been her delight, and sometimes her refuge in times of worry or stress. Out in the sunlight, working with her hands, she turned off the world for a while.

Don found her there in the mid-afternoon, warm and contented with a bag of weeds beside her and the well-appointed rows of vegetables in front of her.

"Hey, let's take a walk down to the coffee shop," he said. "We can do things like that now that I'm retired."

"Okay," she replied. "I'll be ready in about half an hour."

"Half an hour!" Don exclaimed. "Why not now?"

"Look at me. I'm a mess—dirty and sticky. I can't go out for coffee looking like this! Just give me time to shower and dress. It won't take long."

Don shrugged and walked away. "So much for spontaneity," he remarked.

———

One afternoon their daughter Callie drove up in front of the house and bounced up the steps. As usual, Don was relaxing on the front porch.

"Hi Dad. How are you?"

"Fine, thanks. How are you?"

"Very well. Are you still enjoying retirement?"

"Yes, definitely." He paused. "I wish your mother wasn't so busy. I had no idea she did so much work around the house and yard. Whenever I suggest going someplace, she's in the middle of cooking or gardening or whatever."

"Perhaps you need to give her some warning," suggested Callie. "It's hard to drop an activity in the middle of doing it."

"But I really wanted to be spontaneous."

Callie entered the house and found her mother in the kitchen. She noticed the rows of jam jars cooling on the counter.

Helen placed two cups of coffee and a plate of oven-warm cookies on the table, and they sat down to visit.

"Dad seems to have taken up permanent residence on the front porch. Does he ever move?" Callie laughed.

"Sometimes he goes to the coffee shop with the other retired men," replied Helen with a sigh.

"What about you, Mom? You hoped to spend more time together once Dad retired."

"He retired, but I can't. I still have work to do. I suggested to your dad that if he helped me with the housework, I would have more time to go places with him."

"What did he say?"

Helen gave a sarcastic smile. "He reminded me that he was retired and didn't do any work."

Callie sipped her coffee slowly. "Mom, you should retire, too. You've earned it."

"But it's not possible. The housework and yard work still need to be done."

"I don't agree, Mom. You can make it possible. Cut down on what you do. Your children have left home, but you're still doing enough gardening, cooking, canning, and jam-making to feed the army. You give most of it away. And you don't need to wash down the walls every spring, or keep the furniture polished to a high lustre. And you certainly don't need to sew your own curtains."

"I suppose I could do less," said Helen thoughtfully. "I really do want to spend more time with your father." She sat in silence for a few minutes as she considered the possibilities. Then she smiled, her eyes sparkling. "I'll do it. I'll retire."

That evening, as Helen cleaned the kitchen, she told Don, "Since you're enjoying retirement so much, I've decided to retire, too, starting tomorrow."

"But you don't have a job. How can you retire?" asked Don with surprise.

"I'm going to retire anyway. You've made it sound so attractive that I want it, too."

The next morning, Helen arose early to her first day of retirement. Still wearing her housecoat, she poured herself a glass of orange juice and carried it to the front porch. She sat down on the lounge chair and put her feet up.

While sipping her juice, she thought over her plan: she would stop doing housework and yard work. When Don questioned her, she would simply tell him she had retired. When he got the message that she wasn't planning to do any more work, she would tell him she was giving up the nonessential work and would hired a housekeeper to do the rest. The alternative would be that he could help her do the chores in order to free up her time for the retirement activities.

While she relaxed on the porch, she enjoyed the view of the front yard. The bushes and flowers she had planted bloomed in the warm summer morning. Strange that she had only looked at them at close range, when she'd been planting or weeding. It was good to sit still and just enjoy them this way.

She was still savouring the scene when Don came out of the house.

"Aren't you going to make breakfast?" he asked.

"No, I'm retired," she stated quietly.

He looked puzzled. Then a broad grin spread across his face. "Well, retired lady, suppose we take a walk in the park. Then maybe we can go out for lunch."

"That sounds good to me." Helen stood and picked up her empty glass.

The walk was refreshing, and the companionship pleasant. Without the distraction of chores and the interference of radio and television, Helen and Don talked of many topics they had long ignored. Helen learned how tired Don had really been on the job, and how discouraged he had often felt when plans he had made didn't come to fruition.

"Things are changing too fast for me to keep up with them," he said. "It's no one's fault. Businesses have to keep up, otherwise they lose. But I'm glad to be out of it."

For her part, Helen realized she hadn't been to the park since the children were small. Had she got herself into a household rut?

They wandered through the farmers market, admiring the products in some stalls and making a few purchases in others. They ate a leisurely lunch at the Chicken Shack. Afterward they strolled through their town's business district.

As they walked, Don hesitantly voiced a topic that had been on his mind since the early morning when he had discovered breakfast unprepared, the living room untidy, and the bed unmade.

"Helen, I want you to know that I appreciate all the work you've done taking care of the house and the children all these years. Other men go home to messy houses. They have to prepare meals or pick up their children. You made it easy for me. I didn't have to do those things. I could focus on my job, then relax at home. Thank you."

"I'm glad you told me. I often wondered if you noticed anything I did," replied Helen with a smile.

"Yes, I did, and I'm sorry I didn't tell you before," he said. "Now that you're retired, have you any plans on how we should handle the house chores?"

Helen made a mental note of the *we* in his question. "Yes, I have. First, I intend to cut down. Callie pointed out that I was doing too much unnecessary work—"

"So Callie has been giving you the gears, too," he interrupted. "She also made it plain to me that I should help you."

Helen laughed at the thought of her daughter's persuasion. "I would appreciate that. It will be a new life for both of us."

"What if we set aside two days a week to do the chores together?" Don asked. "And now, what would you like to do to celebrate the rest of your first day of retirement? Dinner? A movie? Takeout food?"

Helen sighed with contentment. "This has been a good day. I've learned a few lessons about taking it easy and enjoying the present. I'm ready to go home now. Since we had a big lunch, we won't need much for supper. I could make some sandwiches."

"I'll make the sandwiches," replied Don with a smile. "Today is your day of leisure."

2.

RELUCTANT BRIDESMAID

THE PHONE WAS RINGING AS I OPENED MY EYES. I MUTTERED a couple of curses as I got up to answer it. With the day off from work, I had hoped to sleep in.

"Hello, Bethany. How are you?" said a sweet voice I recognized very well.

"I'm fine, thank you. How are you, Joanne?"

"So it's still Joanne, not Mom," she said in a disappointed tone.

I wasn't taken in by her remark. As far as I was concerned, the woman had no feelings, had no love for anyone but her own precious self.

"No, it's Joanne. Charlene is my mother now." I was still annoyed at being wakened early on a sleep-in day. "So how long has it been? About two years since you last called? To what do I owe this honour?"

"I was hoping you would come and visit this fall. I'm going to be married on October 14."

"Congratulations," I said without enthusiasm. There had been Dad, then three lovers after that. Did she really expect to get it right this time?

"Thank you. Will you come? I want you and Megan to be my bridesmaids."

I was on the point of giving a brusque refusal when an idea popped into my mind. "I'll have to think about it, Joanne. I'll have to check my work schedule. Then I'll let you know."

"All right then. I hope you can make it. Goodbye."

That afternoon, I went to visit my sister, Megan.

"Did Joanne call you? You know she's getting married," I said as soon as I was seated on the couch with my month-old niece sleeping on my lap.

"Yes, she phoned and asked me to be in her wedding party. I told her it was out of the question. Trevor can't get off work, and I can't travel so far alone with a new baby and a one-year-old. What about you? Are you going?"

"I said I'd have to check my schedule," I replied.

"So, you might go! Really!"

"I might," I said. "Probably not."

Megan picked up her toddler. "I would consider it if she lived closer, but I'm not putting myself out to make such a long drive."

While she carried the little guy to his room for a nap, I picked up a photo from the table. It showed Megan and me, ages eight and six, well-scrubbed and well-dressed, with beautiful hair. Joanne liked beautiful clothes and beautiful décor—nothing but the best for her. It was probably the last photo of us before she'd walked out on her husband and children.

"I can just imagine the wedding," I remarked to Megan, who had returned to the room. "The dresses, the flowers, the decorations—it will be perfection."

"There's nothing wrong with that," said Megan, smiling. "I know you would prefer to wear jeans or sweats."

"Dad wasn't perfect enough for her. Neither were we." I was determined to enjoy my resentment.

"I know marriages break up, but the way she did it..." Megan sighed. "She left when Dad was in the hospital, fighting for his life, dumped us at Aunt Terri's place, cleaned out the bank account, and took everything else."

"How many times did she promise to come and see us or take us to visit, then not show up? That was the most hurtful part. I used to wonder if there was something wrong with us, if she didn't love us. Remember the Mother's Day when she didn't come?" Once again I felt anger rising in me. "But you don't seem bothered by it."

Megan, as usual, was unperturbed.

"I refuse to let our past memories spoil the present," replied Megan quietly. "I have so much. I have Trevor and the babies. I have you and Dad and Charlene, Aunt Terri and Uncle Max, Grandma and Grandpa. I am choosing to focus on them, not on our runaway mother."

I remembered Dad struggling. He had moved us back to his hometown while he got our lives in order. He had started a new job, settled us in school, and a few months later found us a permanent place to live. He'd realized that his wife had rejected him, not us, because she hadn't wanted a man with health problems.

"I was glad when Dad married Charlene," continued Megan. "She gave us a normal family life."

"And she loved us," I added tenderly. Dad had made a really good choice of a wife.

"We were the children she never had."

I nodded, pulling my thoughts back to the present. Now our ex-mother was getting married and wanted us at her convenience, to dress us up in beautiful clothes and put on a show. There was really no good reason I should bother going to her wedding—no reason at all.

The next day, I phoned her.

"I can get off work, so I'm coming to your wedding," I told her.

"I'm so glad, dear. When will you arrive?"

"Probably around midnight on the thirteenth. I'll stay overnight at a hotel so you won't have to wait up for me."

"But you'll miss the wedding rehearsal," she complained. "And how can we get your dress fitted?"

"It can't be helped," I explained. "I have to work on the thirteenth. Then it's a six-hour drive to your place."

"Can you come for a visit sometime before then, so we can work on your dress?"

"No, I can't. It's just too far. Mail the dress to me, and Aunt Terri can help me make the adjustments."

"I suppose that's the only choice we have. I'll send the dress. I'll see you on the morning of the fourteenth. And Bethany," she added tenderly, "I'm so glad you're going to be my bridesmaid."

On the morning of the wedding day, my cell phone rang early. It was Joanne.

"Will you come over soon, so we can do your hair and your nails?" she asked. She was still a perfectionist mother. Nothing but the finest for her pretty wedding!

"I can't," I said bluntly. "I didn't get away last night, so I'll have to drive today."

"What!" she exclaimed with alarm. "Bethany, how could you? What about your hair and your nails? The ceremony starts at two-thirty."

"It couldn't be helped. I had to work late, then I was too tired to drive. I can make it on time, but you'll have to put up with a bridesmaid with crummy nails and bad hair. See you later!"

I smiled with satisfaction as I thought of ruining her lovely plans. It was fun to make her squirm.

The phone rang again at two o'clock, then at two-fifteen, at two-twenty, and at two-thirty. That time it rang—and rang—and rang. It rang again at two-forty-five and again at three o'clock.

The next day, Megan called.

"I was thinking of you yesterday. How was the wedding?"

"I don't know," I replied. "I didn't go."

"What do you mean, you didn't go?" said Megan in a puzzled tone. "After planning to be in the wedding party, you didn't even go?"

"That's right! I gave her a taste of her own medicine. I did to her what she did to us so many times."

"Beth, you didn't!" she exclaimed. "You mean you planned all along not to show up?"

"That's right," I said smugly. "It was fun. Revenge is sweet."

Megan grew serious. "I can't blame you for your feelings, but please don't do it again."

"Why not?"

"Listen to me. Our mother hurt us by not being part of our lives, and by making promises she didn't keep. It sounds like fun to take revenge, but I don't want to be like her; I don't want you to be like her either."

"Oh, I see." I paused for a moment. "You don't want me to be a liar and a sneak."

"No, I don't. And I don't like you wallowing in self-pity either. Do the smart thing—quit allowing her to control your feelings."

"Then what do you suggest I do, big sister?"

"If she asks you for anything, just give an honest yes or no. Don't pull any more tricks. You don't have to be like that."

"Okay, I won't."

The next day, I mailed the bridesmaid's dress back to Joanne. I was tempted to cut it into pieces, the way she had cut up our lives, but I remembered Megan's advice. I really didn't want a life of dirty tricks.

3.

LISA'S LEGACY

CURTIS MULLEN AWOKE WITH THE MORNING SUN STREAMING in his bedroom window. Once again his sleep had been disturbed. It was always the same nightmare—Lisa's face haunting him from the shadows of death. On those rare nights when he didn't dream, sleep gave him a few peaceful hours of forgetfulness.

He heard the sound of the tractor in the yard outside. His father was up at dawn, just like his father and grandfather who had farmed this land before him. Curt knew that someday he would take over the place. In the meantime, his job with a building contractor provided useful experience, as well as money in his bank account.

When Curt walked into the kitchen, his mother Diane was talking on the telephone. With the receiver still in hand, she turned to him and said, "Melanie wants to know if you could give Danielle a ride home after you finish work. She's staying late at school to work on a project, so she can't take the bus."

"Of course," he replied. "Tell her to expect me around five o'clock."

Danielle meant a lot to him. She was his niece, his sister Melanie's daughter. Only four years younger than he was, she seemed more like a sister. They had been play-mates as children and remained close friends now that they were older.

"Yes, he'll pick her up at school at five," Diane spoke into the phone.

"Mom, after I drive Danielle home, I'm going to Grandma's place," Curt said. "I promised to repair the rail-ing on her deck, so I won't be home for supper."

He filled a plate with ham and eggs, poured himself a glass of orange juice, and sat down at the table.

As they ate breakfast, Curt asked, "Have you noticed that Danielle seems to be very tense lately?"

"Yes, I have," Diane said. "I really think it has a lot to do with her boyfriend."

"Tyson Harker—he's no good! I wish she'd wise up and get rid of him."

"I agree with you." Diane was thoughtful for a moment, then sighed. "It's hard to tell that to a young girl in love."

With these thoughts still in mind, Curt headed out to the yard and climbed into his truck. Danielle had teased him about buying the truck. "Is it a male thing, buying an old truck and spending a fortune to repair it?" she had asked.

He had patiently explained to her that farmers repaired their own vehicles; they didn't waste money paying others to do it. Besides, a truck was more useful to him than a car.

He drove down the gravel road which led from the farm to the paved highway, carefully staying to the speed limit. How he wished he had always been this careful. As he reached it, he stopped long enough to check for traffic from both directions before proceeding. Curt never passed this corner without reliving the accident.

It had happened three years ago on a Friday evening. After racing his truck along the gravel road, he had casually glanced in both directions as the setting sun obscured his vision, then impatiently pulled out onto the highway. In the next instant, he'd felt the jolt and heard the crash of vehicle against vehicle.

The next few minutes had passed in a daze. He'd seen Lisa Alexander slumped on the passenger seat, Jonathan Rayne shakily climbing out the door on the driver's side. The police and the ambulance had arrived. The police had tested him for alcohol consumption and taken his statement. The attendants had lifted Lisa onto a stretcher, then loaded her into the back of the ambulance. Then he'd heard the scream of the siren.

The police had informed him later that Lisa had died before reaching the hospital; Jonathan had been treated for minor injuries. They'd charged Curt with reckless driving causing death.

The accident made for a lot of talk, not surprising in a small farming community. Both the Mullens and Alexanders had lived in the area for four generations. The funeral had been held in the community hall, as the church hadn't been large enough to hold the anticipated crowd. Lisa's brother sang a solo. Her sister had read a tender eulogy. Curt had attended the funeral, along with his mother and father. He would rather have stayed away. His own remorse and the condemnation he'd expected from others weighed heavily upon him.

The condemnation had never materialized; neither had the hard feelings between families, thanks to Lisa's parents. They had chosen to be forgiving. They'd communicated to his lawyer that Curtis Mullen was a young man of good character who had never caused any trouble before in his life. They had made it plain that they wouldn't seek revenge; they requested that the judge be merciful in his sentencing.

In the end, Curt had been found guilty and sentenced to several hours of community service. His true punishment, he realized, was the sense of regret and guilt he had carried with him every day since the accident.

After work, Curt drove to the school. As Danielle climbed into the truck, he noticed that she seemed tired and anxious. Where was the relaxed, friendly girl he knew?

"I'm glad you were able to pick me up," said Danielle.

"No problem."

"I needed to talk to you privately."

He looked at her curiously. "What about?"

"I'm pregnant." Then in a rush, she explained, "Tyson said to keep it a secret. He plans to drive me to a clinic next Thursday. Of course, it means skipping school without Mom and Dad's permission. I'll get in trouble for that. He says if I don't get rid of it, we're through." Her eyes filled with tears and she started to sob. "He could have been kinder. He used to be very sweet, but now I'm seeing a nasty side to him."

Curt said nothing. What was there to say? He reflected that he would like to beat up that useless Tyson—getting a girl pregnant, taking no responsibility, threatening her, binding her to secrecy.

Danielle dried her tears, blew her nose, and composed herself. "Curt, are you going to tell anyone?"

"I don't know," he replied quietly. "I'll have to think about it."

Later, Curt had plenty of time to think as he repaired his grandmother's deck. He pounded the nails with unusual vigour.

"The jerk!" he said out loud.

"Who are you calling a jerk?" asked Grandma as she opened the door.

"Someone who deserves it."

"Really." Grandma raised an eyebrow. "Supper will be ready in a couple of minutes. Suppose you come in now."

While Grandma finished her supper preparations, Curt glanced through a stack of brochures on the shelf beside the door.

"Grandma, why do you go to all these meetings and give to all these causes?"

"Oh, I don't know. It's important to me to make the world a better place. I hope I can do some good—even though I am too old to be very useful."

"May I take these two?" asked Curt. "I know someone who should read them."

She glanced at the titles: *Six Reasons Not to Have an Abortion* and *Adoption: A Better Alternative*. "Not your girlfriend, I hope," she remarked.

"No, they're for someone else. Besides, I don't have a girlfriend."

Curt didn't have time to read the brochures until the next evening.

Abortion is a lot more complicated than I realized, he thought as he scanned *Six Reasons*.

He still had the brochures in his hand when he sat down at the supper table.

Joe Mullen looked curiously at his son's reading material and nearly choked on a sip of coffee. "Where did you get those?" he sputtered.

"From Grandma," replied Curt. "Two of her many pamphlets."

"But why the sudden interest in—that? You've never mentioned it before," said Diane.

Curt drew a deep breath. "Because Danielle is pregnant, and her boyfriend is arm-twisting her into a secret abortion."

"Irresponsible trash!" exclaimed Joe. "When I was young, if a man got his girlfriend pregnant, he married her and took responsibility. The boys nowadays are just babies!"

"Not all of us, Dad. Don't give all of us a bad name because of a loser like Tyson Harker."

"What does Danielle think?" asked Diane.

"She's pretty upset. She also feels betrayed by Tyson's threats."

"She confided in you. That means she isn't keeping it a secret anymore," Diane observed.

"She asked if I was going to tell anyone. I said I wasn't sure." Curt hesitated a moment. He thought about his own untimely birth to a forty-year-old mother. "I've never heard you folks talk about abortion. Why didn't you?"

"It didn't seem necessary," replied Joe. "To be honest, I thought having babies—or not having them—was a woman's concern."

"Except that the woman needs a man in the first place, if she gets pregnant," remarked Diane with a note of sarcasm. "Are you going to say anything more to Danielle about it, Curt?"

"Yes, I'm going to let her know that she and Tyson can't do this in secret. I plan to tell everyone I know that she's pregnant. Maybe I can save this child's life."

"So you don't agree with, ah—getting rid of it," said Joe.

"Look at it this way. It's murder to kill a baby after it's born. Why isn't it murder to kill it before?"

Diane smiled. "That's our opinion, too."

"What about Melanie and Gordon? What do they think? Will they encourage her to have the baby, or have an abortion?"

"I don't know," said his mother sadly. "We never discussed issues like this with Melanie either."

"They are definitely going to read Grandma's pamphlets," remarked Curt. "This abortion business is a lot harder than it's made out to be."

Diane spoke hesitantly. "Curt, you never discuss the accident, but I can't help wondering if this has anything to do with Lisa's death."

"Maybe it does. If anything, the accident taught me that life is precious. It also taught me that life can be easily ended. I can't just stand by and say nothing while this child's life is taken away."

"I see your point, but will talking Danielle out of it make you feel any better about Lisa?"

"Probably not, but I don't want to feel worse."

The next morning dawned grey and rainy. Puddles were scattered all over the yard. Curt's boss phoned to say they wouldn't be working on account of the weather.

Curt considered his plans for the day. He would help his dad in the machine shed and perhaps change the oil in his truck. It would also be a good day to talk to Danielle again.

He phoned early, before she left for school.

"Hi Danielle," he said. "How would you like to go out and have a snack with your favourite uncle? I could pick you up after school."

"Yes, I'd like that," she replied. "See you later."

That afternoon, they both sat at a booth in the coffee shop, Curt with pie and coffee and Danielle with a cherry swirl. Curt was uncomfortable; he had rehearsed several times the words he wanted to say, but the message wouldn't come out as he had intended.

He took a deep breath and tried a different course. "Danielle, will you do something for me, something very special?"

"Maybe. It depends what it is."

"Will you give me your child?"

"Curt, what do you mean? Do you want to take the child and raise it?" she answered with surprise.

"No, that isn't what I mean. I'm not a suitable person for that, a young single man. What I'm asking you to do is let the baby live. Don't let Tyson railroad you into an abortion."

Danielle smiled. Curt noticed that she seemed relaxed for the first time in months. "Tyson will have nothing to do with my decision," she said. "I dumped him this morning."

"Good for you! You deserve someone better."

"The next time my friends tell me that a boy is no good, I'm going to believe them," she said with a smile. "I feel free for a change. I can decide for myself. I don't want to abort the child, but I don't want to keep it either. I want to go away to college, not stay home with Mom and Dad to look after a baby and probably work a minimum wage job."

"You could put the baby up for adoption," suggested Curt. "There are lots of people who want to adopt. I know it's not an easy decision. There is no easy decision in this whole situation." He took the brochures out of his pocket and pushed them across the table. "A gift from great-grandma. These might help you make up your mind. I hope that when this is over, you can carry on with your life. I don't want you to look back with regret. Life is too valuable for that."

"How true," she said thoughtfully. "I guess the thing to do now is discuss it with Mom and Dad." Then she added resolutely, "Curt, I want you to give up something, too."

"What is that?" he asked with surprise.

"Lisa! Give her up, Curt. Since she was killed, you've been dragging yourself around, all work and no play. You don't see your friends anymore or go out socially. You just said that life is valuable, but you act as if life isn't worth living."

"But it's because of me that Lisa died, and I'll never forget that. I don't ever want you to know what it's like to cause someone's death."

"Okay, you've made your point. You want the baby to have a life. You want me to have a life. But you need a life, too. Everyone else, including Lisa's mom and dad, wants you to have a life. It's time, Curt. Get on with it."

He smiled at her persistence. "Okay. You want a new start for both of us."

On the way home, Curt took an unaccustomed detour; he turned onto the road that led through the cemetery. He found her gravestone easily: Lisa Joy Alexander.

"Well, Lisa," he said aloud. "I would bring you back if I could, but Danielle is right: I have to let you go. This is goodbye." As he walked back to his truck, he knew that the nightmare would no longer control his life.

4.

SECOND-HAND SMOKE, SECOND-HAND LOVE

CAROLYN SAT IN DR. WARDEL'S OFFICE, SILENT FOR A moment, stunned by his suggestion.

"You can't really mean that!" she exclaimed.

"Yes, I do mean it. In order for you to save your life, you should move out."

"How can I do that? How can I leave my husband? Our younger daughter is still at home. What would this do to her?"

"I'm sorry," the doctor said. "But you've been living with second-hand smoke for years. It's killing you. First you had emphysema, now you have lung cancer. We can treat the cancer, but if you continue to live with second-hand smoke, there's a strong chance it will return."

"I have asked Ken to give up smoking several times, but he's refused. He won't go outdoors to smoke either. But I don't want to leave my family." She sighed. "Suppose

I persuade him to restrict his smoking to one room—and I stay out of that room?"

"Yes, that would help. Do anything you can to keep away from smoke."

As she drove home from her appointment, Carolyn considered her only option—persuade Ken to smoke in the rumpus room. Surely he would do that much for her. Why of all things was he so stubborn about smoking? Quitting an addiction was tough, of course, but why wouldn't he even try? He had been a good man in so many ways. He never forgot a birthday or anniversary. They had had so many special times together—family vacations, picnics at the beach. She ignored the hard side as much as possible—the bouts of heavy drinking, the frequent job changes, the unpaid bills, and the constant arguments between him and his brothers.

After parking the car in the driveway, she paused to take the mail out of the box before entering the front door. Their golden retriever, Buffy, trotted over to greet her, tail wagging. Carolyn reached down to give the dog an affectionate pat on her head.

Ken was sitting in an easy chair watching a documentary on television.

"I ordered Chinese food for supper," he said. "I thought you would need a break from cooking after seeing the doctor."

Carolyn nodded politely as she sat on the recliner and put her feet up. She was tired. Her cancer consumed most of her waking thoughts while the treatments tired her body.

She glanced through the mail, which was still in her hand—two flyers, the phone bill, as well as the latest issue of *Pet Digest* with a photo of a border collie on the cover.

"How did your appointment go?" asked Ken.

Carolyn shook her head.

"Is your cancer worse?" he asked with concern.

"No, so far the treatments are proving to be effective, but the doctor doesn't like me living with second-hand smoke." She looked directly at him. "Ken, you don't want to give up smoking and you've refused to go outside to smoke. What if I asked you to limit your smoking to the rumpus room? Would you do it?"

"I don't see why I should have to go downstairs to smoke. We built the rumpus room as a place for the kids to play."

Sixteen-year-old Lacey walked into the room in time to hear her father's explanation. Her worry about her mother had made her sensitive. She was angry at her father's insistence on smoking.

"Dad, why on earth won't you smoke downstairs? It won't hurt you a bit. What's the matter? Don't you love Mom?"

"Yes, I do love your mother," he explained patiently.

"Then why won't you make any changes in your smoking for her? Aren't you afraid of losing her?"

"Listen, Pumpkin. Smoking is not going to make any difference. Those reports connecting smoking with cancer are greatly exaggerated. If they were true, I would be the one who has cancer, not your mother. After all, I'm the one who's been smoking for over thirty years."

Lacey ran to her bedroom in tears.

Ken sighed with exasperation. "Why is she so moody all the time? Amanda was never like that."

"When Amanda was sixteen, she didn't have to deal with her mother having cancer," Carolyn said. "Anyway, I'm going to do everything I can to beat it. Dr. Wardel suggested I move out, but I don't want to do that. I'm sure you don't want it either. Since you won't go downstairs to smoke, I'll have to be the one to move. I'll only use the kitchen to get myself something to eat, otherwise I will live downstairs. You and Lacey will have to do the housework. And you will have to keep your smoking upstairs. Will you go along with that?"

"Sure," he replied.

The following day, with Lacey's help, Carolyn moved her clothes and toiletries downstairs. She put them away in the spare bedroom and bathroom, and on the coffee table she placed the bouquet of pink carnations Ken had given her. Afterward she lay on the couch to rest. Every effort tired her these days. Buffy lay on the carpet beside her. She stroked the dog's smooth fur.

Lacey sat down. "I still don't think it's fair," she exclaimed. "Dad should give up smoking for you. I hid his cigarettes yesterday, but he just went out and bought another pack."

"Hiding his cigarettes won't help, and breaking a habit like smoking is a tough thing to do," replied her mother. "I just wish he would smoke outside or restrict his smoking to one room."

"I wish he would, too. It just seems as if he doesn't love you enough."

Carolyn sighed. She didn't have the energy to deal with this conflict between Ken and Lacey. "You and your dad will have to settle your own arguments. All my effort has to go toward staying alive."

After Lacey had gone upstairs, Carolyn thought of her situation. She was lonely—lonely in her cancer, and worst of all, lonely in her marriage. Would she have to stay in the basement for the rest of her life? She needed Ken's partnership in dealing with her illness; instead he gave flowers, kind words, and Chinese food! She pictured him upstairs with his television, his newspaper, his friends, his relatives, his booze, and his smokes. Had their home ever belonged to her?

She recalled the times when her family and friends had visited; Ken stood awkwardly to one side waiting for them to leave. Although he appreciated the easy camaraderie and quiet respect that her family members showed toward each other, he didn't understand it.

Lacey was a good girl, but still very young and sensitive. What would happen to her if her mother didn't make it?

No! She would not think that way. Recovery was tied up in having a positive attitude, not in the negative drift of her mind. She would focus on getting well and do everything possible to facilitate it.

———

Upstairs, Ken sat down to relax. He lit a cigarette and picked up *Pet Digest*, which was lying on the table where Carolyn had left it. He had taken the subscription many years ago for the children. Yet he and Carolyn also enjoyed reading its helpful articles. If you kept an animal, it was very important to give it the best care.

While Carolyn continued to rest in her place of exile, Ken walked downstairs. She noticed that he appeared agitated. Had he and Lacey argued again?

"How are you and Lacey getting along?" she inquired.

Ken ignored her question. He sat down beside her and handed her the magazine.

"See this article," he said, pointing to the page. "It states that second-hand smoke can cause liver and kidney damage to animals."

He remained silent for a few minutes while she glanced at the article. Then he exclaimed, "I'd never forgive myself if anything happened to Buffy on account of my smoking!"

Carolyn was startled by his exclamation. "What are you going to do about it?"

"I'm going outside for one last cigarette, then I'm going to quit for good." He picked up his half-finished pack of cigarettes and lighter and headed upstairs to the back door.

5.

CHOICES

IT WAS A NORMAL START ON WHAT WAS SUPPOSED TO BE A normal day. We ate breakfast. Dan left for work. I hustled Sarah and Rachel out the door to catch the school bus. Then the phone rang with the message that would bring my world crashing down.

"Hello, Kate," said Mother as soon as I answered. "How are you?"

"Fine. Thanks, Mom. How are you?"

"I'm very well." She paused long enough for me to wonder about it. Mother was usually a bright, talkative person. She continued slowly. "I have some news to tell you. I have moved out of the house. I have left your dad."

I felt as if someone had punched me in the stomach and knocked the wind out of me.

"But Mom, you can't do that!" I said as soon as I caught my breath. "What about our family! What about your home! Don't you care about Jeff and me? Do you really hate Dad that much? I know he's critical, but he doesn't beat you or chase women, or drink heavily or do drugs..."

I was out of breath. This was a major shock.

"Kate, listen to me, and try to understand. I have lived my whole married life with your father trying to change every little thing about me. You and Jeff are on your own; you don't need me anymore. I'm tired of being someone I'm not. I want to be myself."

"I don't want to understand. Why don't you understand what it's like for me? I feel as if I never really had a family, that it was all phony."

"Maybe it was always phony, but the phoniness is over now. I can relax and enjoy life instead of pretending to be something I'm not. I have my own apartment. Would you like to come and see it?"

"No, Mom. Quite frankly I wouldn't. It isn't my home, and I don't want to see it. Have you told Jeff yet?"

"Yes, I called him an hour ago. He was as disappointed as you are. I guess I can't blame either of you, but I've made my decision and I'm going to stick to it."

"Fine, then. Just don't expect me to be happy about it." I banged down the receiver.

Next I called Jeff, my big brother. "What do you think about Mom leaving Dad?" I asked.

"I hate the whole idea. I was thinking of looking for a job closer to home so I could move back near the family. Fifteen hundred miles is a long way off. But now what's the point? There isn't a home to come back to. I feel the way you do, that our family has been ripped away from us."

"But what can we do to get them back together again?"

"Nothing! They have to do it themselves. We're stuck with it."

"Well, if they think I am going to go along and be nice about it, they're in for a disappointment," I exclaimed.

Next I called Dad. "What do you guys think you're doing, busting up your marriage and your family? Don't you love your children? Don't you think this hurts us? Or don't you think at all?"

"Please remember that this was your mother's idea, so don't blame me," explained Dad. Why did he always have to be so analytical? "I don't like it either, and I don't understand what the problem is. She never said. After I gave her everything she wanted, and made a good life for her, she should be grateful."

"Maybe you should be grateful yourself! Maybe you should do something constructive about it instead of always criticising!"

"What can I do if she's determined to stay away?"

I calmed down. "Jeff and I would have a lot more respect for you folks if you worked at solving your problems instead of running away from them. Isn't that what you always advised us to do?"

The next few weeks were a time of grieving. I had no energy or enthusiasm. A dark cloud surrounded my thinking. I woke up in the morning to the shock of my lost family; I went to bed at night depressed.

Dan patiently carried on with life. He saw to the girls' needs, spent all his spare time with them, and drove them to their activities.

"Are you going to ball practice with us?" he asked one evening. I shook my head.

"Isn't Mom ever going with us anywhere again?" asked Sarah.

Dan replied, "Your mother needs time to be alone for a while."

"Okay, but it seems she doesn't want to be our mother anymore."

One afternoon, Dad phoned. "Hi, Katie, how are you?" he asked cheerfully. "Would you like to go for coffee?"

"Yes, I'd like that. But let's not talk about your separation. I really don't want to discuss it."

"Okay. Let's meet at The Muffin Shop. See you around three."

Dad was waiting for me in the parking lot of The Muffin Shop. To my dismay, I saw that he had brought a woman with him. She was about fifty, small and trim, with sparkling eyes and an engaging manner.

"There's someone I want you to meet," said Dad with an embarrassed smile. "This is Mindy Semble. Mindy, this is my daughter, Kate."

"I've really been looking forward to meeting you," Mindy gushed.

I coolly said hello and refused her outstretched hand.

"Well, Dad," I remarked sarcastically, "you could hardly wait to be rid of Mom before you found a replacement for her." I wasn't going to be falsely polite about Dad and his new woman.

Mindy looked as if she had been slapped. The smile vanished from Dad's face. "Now wait a minute, Katie. The separation was your mother's idea, not mine. Am I supposed to be alone the rest of my life just because she wanted out?"

"I don't care whose idea it was. I still think it stinks! You and Mom don't have to be alone; you have each other. If the two of you had any guts, you would solve your problems instead of busting up."

I was yelling now. "What makes you think I should be happy for you now that you've found a little cutie to replace my mother? How remarkable that you found someone who's a lot like she used to be—before you made her over. She was a refreshing, fun person to begin with. After that, she was only fun when you weren't around."

Dad's face grew serious. "You don't need to be insulting."

"And how long is it going to take you to make over this Mindy person into a prim and proper lady who fits into your box? Mom would have a good laugh if you did that!"

"You can tell your mother that—"

"I'm not telling my mother anything from you. You can call her and communicate with her yourself. I'm not your messenger!"

With this parting shot, I jumped in the car and drove away, leaving Dad and his lady friend standing in the parking lot.

I cried all the way home. I was angry at Dad, but I was also ashamed of the way I had lost my temper with him.

Sitting in the kitchen, between sobs and nose-blowing, I poured out my troubles to Dan. He listened in silence, then paused a few minutes before answering. "Kate, listen to me. You have to make a choice here. You're grieving for your lost family. I can't blame you. I would feel the same if my parents split up. But you're poisoning yourself, the girls, and me by focusing on it so completely. We don't have much of a life with you right now. I feel like I'm being two parents, because your time is spent on your own grief. We have a good marriage and a good family life, and I don't want that to change. Choose how you are going to deal with your mom and dad. Then leave them alone to run their own lives."

"That doesn't mean I'll stop being hurt," I said sulkily. But I knew he was right; I wasn't giving any part of myself to him and the girls. They were carrying on without me.

"You're right," Dan said. "The grieving won't stop automatically. But this family needs to get on with life and I'd like it to be with all four of us in the picture."

"Okay. I think I already decided what to do on the way home, but I needed you to make it plain for me. I'm lucky to have a husband like you." I smiled affectionately at him. "Another man would just have walked out. I'm feeling ashamed of the way I treated Dad, and I need to apologize to him."

I stayed up late that evening, at my computer, composing a letter to Mom and Dad.

Dear Mom and Dad,

I have said a lot of nasty things to you both since you split up, and I want you to know that I'm sorry. I had no right to treat you with such disrespect.

I also want to thank you. Yes, I mean it. You gave us a good home, and love and care, all the time we were young, and then you let us get on with our adult lives. I'm glad you stayed together while we were children and teenagers. We didn't have to trot back and forth between two homes. We didn't have to lead a double life the way so many children do.

Now I'm an adult. My life is my responsibility, and the choices I make are mine. The choice I'm making is this: my husband and children come first. Whatever is in the best interests of our family takes priority.

Another choice I'm making is that I refuse to lead a double life as an adult. I and my family will not come to visit you in your homes, although we will welcome you here anytime. We will not listen to complaints about each other and will not carry messages back and forth between the two of you. Furthermore we do not wish to meet any boyfriends/girlfriends, live-ins, or new spouses; we will not attend any second marriages.

Christmas will be coming soon. You are both invited to join us in our home to celebrate with us.

Once again, I'm sorry for all my hurtful remarks. I love you both.

—Kate

I pressed the send button. In the morning, I would show this letter to Dan. Then I would get back to being the wife and mother I used to be.

6.

LEAVING THE NEST

My bags were packed and ready to go. I had filled my backpack and tote bag with the clothing and toiletries I would need for the next few weeks. If Mom had known, she would have repacked them; she had no confidence in my ability to do anything without her help.

I sauntered out to the living room. My canary, Teenie, was singing her heart out. I had bought her four years ago, when I was sixteen. I could have asked Dad's permission to get a bird. He would have given me a definite yes or no. But I had badly wanted the canary, so I asked Mom instead. As usual, she blew the matter out of proportion, talked it to death, then said yes, on the condition that I take care of it. I always got a yes from Mom, as long as I could put up with her ranting.

The first week, I cleaned Teenie's cage every morning. Then on Saturday morning, Mom was up early and decided to clean the cage herself. After that, she took over the bird. I was pleased that Mom liked the canary and her beautiful singing, but I resented the fact that she thought I wasn't competent enough to look after my own pet.

I walked into the kitchen where Mom and Jessica were yapping at each other. My younger sister was the only one who could outtalk Mom, the only one who could get past her constant interrupting. I had learned that the best way to manage my life was not to talk much, especially about problems. The only way for a quiet person like me to compete with a talkative person was to say nothing.

When I first went to college, Mom insisted that I take business administration. There would be good job opportunities, she claimed. To be honest, she thought that working in an office was a clean and prestigious way to earn a living, a place to meet respectable people.

I lasted until Christmas. Being cooped up in an office environment, sitting all day at a desk or a computer, distressed me. So I left college, and a few weeks later Mr. Hargraves, the pharmacist who lived next door, offered me a part-time job clerking in his store. Even though I'm shy, I'm also sociable. I enjoyed meeting the customers. It was a good experience for me. My confidence grew every day.

Mom wasn't pleased I had taken a job. "Listen, Rebecca, I don't like the idea of you working in a store. When young people get the feel of money in their pockets, they don't want any more education."

Why didn't she understand that the reason I wanted to go to college in the first place was so I wouldn't have to spend the rest of my life earning minimum wage? The store job gave me the opportunity to earn money for my education—money my mother couldn't control.

I agreed to return to college that fall, but only if I could choose my own course. After discussing my options with the college counsellor, I registered for nursing. I told Mom and Dad after completing my registration. That way, Mom couldn't argue me out of it. In the end, she was appeased by the fact that nurses earn a good salary.

I intended to return to my job at the drug store for the summer after my first year in nursing, but another opportunity presented itself.

One day, as I was eating lunch in the college cafeteria, Candace Greaves sat down at the table with me.

"Hi, Rebecca, how are your courses going?" she asked.

"Really well. I like nursing so much better than business. How about you?"

"I'm doing fine. So the change agreed with you?"

"Yes, it did." I remembered Candace's many activities in high school. "Have you found another yearbook to edit?"

"No, I haven't, and I'm not looking for anything like that. My courses demand too much of my time. Would you be interested in a summer job?"

"I plan to go back to my job at the drug store," I replied, "but I'd consider another opportunity. Do you know of something?"

"My uncle, Nate Rainer, manages Lake Clearwater Camp. I'm going to work for him for the summer. He still needs more staff. If you're interested, I could introduce you to him."

"Yes, I would like that," I said quietly. Inside I was thrilled for the opportunity to live and work at Clearwater Camp for the summer. It would be a new experience! Something different! A chance to spread my wings and fly away from home for a few weeks!

That evening I spoke to Mom.

"I talked to Candace Greaves at lunch," I said. "She's taking a summer job at Lake Clearwater Camp."

"Oh, that Candace! She thinks she's so important. She edited the school yearbook, and stuck her name in everywhere."

Jessica turned to Mom and demanded, "Why do you always criticize everyone we have anything to do with? Is nobody ever good enough for you?"

I walked out of the room to avoid the argument which was sure to follow. I wondered how an editor who took part in so many activities could avoid including her name in the yearbook write-ups. Why couldn't Mom see that? Why was she so determined to tear down other people's achievements?

Candace set up an appointment for me, and two days later I met with Nate Rainer.

"I see from your application that you're taking nursing," he said. "Do you have first aid training?"

"Yes, I do."

"Good. We have a nurse at camp. You can be her assistant, but you'll be required to do several other things. On registration day we need everyone to help. Then there's cabin and activity supervision. How are you at cooking?"

I laughed. "Not very experienced."

"Okay, then we won't assign you to the kitchen. We start on June 29 and continue to August 15. Meals and accommodation are included. I'm prepared to offer you the job now."

"I would be happy to accept," I replied.

That evening, while Mom was driving Jessica to her dance lesson, I sat beside Dad while he read the newspaper.

"Dad, would you mind if I didn't work at the drug store this summer?" I asked. "Would it be okay if I took another job instead?"

"Do whatever you think is best," he replied briefly as he turned the page. Dad was no more of a talker than I was.

The next day I told Candace the news. She was delighted that I had gotten the job. "It will be such fun working together at camp. I was nervous about going, since I don't know any of the staff except Uncle Nate. I'll be glad to have a friend with me."

A friend! That felt good. I didn't make friends easily. It would be great to hang out with a friendly, genuine girl like Candace.

Even so, I felt uneasy about leaving home for the summer. If Mom knew, she would play on my uncertainties and sabotage my plans. I decided not to tell her.

I quietly planned what to pack. Mr. Rainer had told me to bring a pair of rubbers and comfortable outdoor clothing. I would be issued two camp t-shirts. Transportation was settled easily; Candace's father was driving her to the camp and had offered me a ride with them. We would leave Friday afternoon at 1:30.

On Friday morning, after returning some books to the library and picking up a can of insect repellent, I stopped to see Dad at his office. I hoped he wasn't busy, as I wanted a chance to talk. Fortunately he was available, and able to visit.

I sat down and cleared my throat. "Dad, I've accepted a job at Lake Clearwater Camp. I'm leaving this afternoon at 1:30 and will be gone for seven weeks."

Dad looked surprised. He was silent for a few minutes and I began to feel uncomfortable. He had said I could take another job, but maybe he didn't want me to leave home.

"Dad, are you okay with this, or do you want me to stay home?" I asked anxiously.

He spoke slowly. "No, I think you should take the job. You're ready for it. I'm just not ready to have you leave home. You and Jessica have grown up so fast." He smiled sadly. "Have you talked to your mother about this?"

"No, I haven't. I'm going to tell her this afternoon when I'm ready to walk out the door. That way, she can't ruin my plans."

Dad nodded. "I don't blame you," he said thoughtfully. "I have an idea. I'll take your mother out for a late lunch and tell her myself. That way, you can leave when she isn't in the house, so she can't get in a stew about it."

"You mean just sneak out on her?"

"Yes," he said, laughing.

"Thanks, Dad," I said. What I really wanted to say was, *Thanks for understanding; thanks for trusting me; thanks for knowing that I don't have to talk a mile a minute to be successful in life; thanks for knowing that I can make a good decision.*

I stood up to leave. Dad wasn't the demonstrative type, but he put his arms around me and hugged me tightly.

"Rebecca, I want you to know that you're a fine young girl, and I'm proud of you." Tears filled my eyes. As I brushed them away, Dad added, "You realize that your mother loves you and would do anything to help you, even if she isn't always wise."

That afternoon I carried my bags to the front door. I saw Candace and her father pull into the driveway. I walked over to Teenie's cage and whistled along with her.

"Goodbye, little birdie," I said. "Keep Mom happy with your songs."

I picked up my bags and walked out the door.

7.

A WEDDING ON THE BEACH

Matthew Felcher and Tina Kane are pleased to announce their engagement and forthcoming marriage. The wedding will take place on Saturday, July 14 at 11:00 a.m. on the beach at Lake Silvermoon. The reception will follow at Lakeview Hotel.

JOE SELANSKI LOOKED AT THE ANNOUNCEMENT AND THE smiling photo of the happy couple and threw down the newspaper with disgust.

He walked into the bathroom and looked at his reflection in the mirror. He wasn't unhappy with the image he saw there. At age forty, he was tall and sturdy; his body was toned from the physical labour that had been a major part of his livelihood. Most gratifying of all, he had a thick head of hair. Was there something about him that was particularly unattractive or lacking in masculinity?

He remembered the days of his youth, when he had worked in a lumber yard. The small farm he owned hadn't provided a sufficient income. He had needed the job...

———

The job and the farm kept Joe very busy. He wasn't too busy, however, to notice the pretty little clerk who worked at the supply desk. He wasn't too busy to ask her out, or to notice that she seemed as interested in him as he was in her.

That was the start of a beautiful relationship. Two years later, they were married. Life with his pretty wife was delightful. It was made more delightful by the arrival of their two children.

With the arrival of the babies, Joe made a decision regarding the farm. It took too much time to operate, and some of the machinery needed to be replaced. He chose to rent out the land and sell the equipment. The family could live in a house in the city, eliminating the twenty-mile commute.

It was a good life, with their family and friends and work. The children grew. They attended school. Joe thought life couldn't get any better; he was a very lucky man.

One day Tina dropped her bombshell. They were at home together on a Saturday afternoon. Landen and Shaelie were visiting their grandparents.

"Joe, I have something to tell you." She hesitated. "I want you to move out of the house. I don't love you any longer. I want a divorce."

"But darling, why? If there's anything you want from me, or anything you want me to do differently, I'll do it. I'll do anything to make you happy. But please don't say it's over," he pleaded.

"It's too late to change anything. And it's really not your fault, Joe." She plunged ahead. "I don't love you anymore. I love Matt."

Joe felt as if he had been stabbed in the heart. He turned abruptly away from her and spoke angrily. "Right now, Tina, you had better get out of here fast. Go to a hotel. I have never hit a woman in my life, but just now I feel like beating you to a pulp."

Tina left the house immediately, and the next day Joe and the children moved to the farm. Hopefully Tina would get over this stupid crush on Matt "Baldy" Felcher. What did she see in him anyway? He was inclined to overweight, and very paunchy. Most amusing to Joe was his baldness—and the small amount of hair that he kept meticulously shaved.

Besides, why did Matt want to leave his own wife? She was a nice-looking woman, a pleasant person. Moreover, she kept their active twin boys under control. Why did he want to steal someone else's wife when he had a good wife of his own?

The whole situation hurt and puzzled Joe. His pain only increased over the months that followed, as Tina

continued living with Matt and made no attempt to rec-
oncile with Joe.

One day Joe's frustration reached an unbearable peak.
He walked into the neighbourhood church and found the
pastor in his office. After pouring out his hurt and anger,
he exclaimed, "How can I make her come back?"

"You have to let her go," stated the pastor calmly.

"What do you mean? It's not right, it's not fair. We
were supposed to be married for life. I thought you would
be on my side."

"I agree that it's not right," said Pastor Ron. "But
there's no way you can force her to come back to you. If,
in the course of time, she changes her mind, you have the
option of taking her back, but the best thing for you to do
now is to let her go and plan your life without her."

That night, Joe wept bitter tears of loss and heartache.
The next day, he signed the separation agreement.

———

Three years passed. Landen, at age fifteen, had grown to
be a sturdy lad. At thirteen, Shaelie's lean frame was filling
out into adolescent chubbiness.

And now, the delightful couple were to be married.
At Lake Silvermoon, of course! Joe had seen the advertising—a lovely place to be married outdoors amid the beauty
of nature. The children were to be in the wedding party,
as well as Matt's boys. All four children would spend a

wonderful time at the lake with their parents the day before the ceremony.

The romantic wedding on the beach, with the water gently lapping over the feet of the bridal party, would probably have proceeded without incident except for one fact: the children took sick. On Thursday morning before the wedding, Landen woke up with a fever and nausea. All that day he made frequent trips to the bathroom to disgorge the contents of his stomach. The rest of the time he lay down and rested, too weak to do anything else.

On Friday his stomach settled, although he was still weak and feverish. Shaelie, however, woke up to the same symptoms her brother had.

Joe took stock of the situation. No way could they spend the day at the lake with any degree of health and enjoyment. He phoned Tina.

"Tina, I have two sick kids here. Landen was throwing up all yesterday, and now Shaelie has started."

"But we were planning to have a family photo taken this morning," Tina complained. "And I wanted to spend the day with them at the lake."

"They're in no shape to go with you," Joe said. "Tell you what. They want to be with you at your wedding. So tomorrow morning, if they're better, I will drive them to the lake myself."

"Okay, have them here by nine o'clock if you can. They will need to get dressed."

The next morning, Landen's normal good health had returned, but Shaelie, although her stomach had settled, was still weak and tired.

"How do you feel, honey? Are you up to going to the lake?" asked Joe.

"I really want to go, Dad, but I don't feel very well. What should I do? I hate to miss the wedding."

"I'll drive you and Landen to the lake. Then I'll stick around in case you want to come home early. Is that all right with you?"

She smiled with relief and nodded.

At the Lakeview Hotel, they found Tina's room. Joe explained that Shaelie still didn't feel well, so he would hang around the parking lot in case she wanted to leave early. Tina accepted this plan somewhat ungraciously.

Two hours later, the wedding party emerged from the hotel, attired for the ceremony. Joe, sitting on a bench with a cup of coffee, watched with interest. Tina looked petite and lovely in her exquisite gown and veil. Shaelie's hair had been curled, and it framed her sweet face; but her ruffled pink dress turned her chubbiness into gross overweight. An artful application of cosmetics didn't completely hide her pallor or listlessness.

Joe was concerned. The little girl didn't look well. He had better keep an eye on her.

The wedding party walked down the hill to the beach and took their places standing in the shallow water at the edge of the lake while Dan Kirshner, the marriage commissioner, stood on the dry sand.

As the ceremony started, Joe reflected that it felt strange to be witnessing the marriage of his ex-wife. If it were not for Shaelie, he would go.

The wedding proceeded uneventfully, save for repeated attempts to quiet Matt's boys, Ben and Caleb. The ceremony headed to its appropriate conclusion, with the bridal couple holding hands and gazing lovingly into each other's eyes as the marriage commissioner solemnly stated, "By the power vested in me, I now pronounce..."

"I'm going to be sick," exclaimed Shaelie suddenly. She burped, heaved, and spewed vomit all over her pink ruffles, over the back of her mother's snowy white gown, and over lovely Lake Silvermoon.

Joe raced down the hill to his daughter's side as her mother turned.

"Honey, you're not well enough to be here," Joe said. "Go and change your clothes and I'll take you home."

As the pale girl turned toward the hotel, Dan cleared his throat. "We have to finish the ceremony," he said quietly. Tina rearranged her eyes and her smile as she turned to face Matt again. "I now pronounce you husband and wife. You may kiss the bride."

Joe impulsively threw his arms around Tina and planted an intense, lingering kiss on her lips. A few of the guests giggled nervously at this unexpected turn of events.

Matt was outraged. "That's my wife you're kissing!" he yelled.

Joe loosened his embrace and looked at the offended groom. "Matt Felcher, you did this—and much more—to my wife."

"Jerk!" exclaimed Matt as he pushed Joe roughly.

Joe lost his balance, bumped into Tina, and toppled them both into the water.

This time the whole group roared with laughter. Ben and Caleb took advantage of the distraction to release their pent-up energy. They started playing and splashing in the lake. They splashed even more water on the unfortunate bride.

Joe picked himself up amidst the hilarity. Tina stood up as straight and dignified as her five-foot-nothing frame would allow. She wasn't laughing; she was dripping—and furious!

"You oaf," she screamed at Joe. "Did you come here to ruin our wedding? You miserable jackass! You clumsy ox!" She stopped, having run out of breath and profanity.

Joe stifled his laughter. After all, she was the mother of his children, and he and Shaelie had done a pretty good job of messing up her special day. "No, I didn't come here to ruin your wedding. I came because our little girl was sick. I'm sorry I kissed you; it was really out of line. But I'm out of here now. I won't intrude any longer."

He left the wedding party and guests to straighten themselves out as best they could, and climbed the hill toward the hotel. He indulged in his laughter along the way. It relieved him of the resentment he carried toward Tina. He no longer hated Baldy; he wasn't worth hating. The man was too pitiful, with his shaved head and double standard on marriage.

Joe also reflected on his own future. Maybe he would have a wife again, when the children were older. Maybe he would find a real woman who wouldn't run out on him.

Maybe they would have a wedding on the beach.

$8.$
A PLACE FOR THE CHILD

IT WAS A LEISURELY SATURDAY AFTERNOON IN THE SUTTON household. April and her three-year-old son Nathan rolled around together on the floor in a mock wrestling match while baby Anna clapped her hands and laughed with delight. These times of playing with the children were precious to April.

Her husband Richard wasn't at home to enjoy the family fun; he would return later in the afternoon.

A cloud had moved over April's perfect contentment, a tension between herself and her husband. The cause was an eight-year-old boy she had never met.

Before they had married, Richard told her of his past involvement. "There's something I want you to know," he said. "I have a child, a little boy."

"Where does he live?" she asked.

"He lives with his mother. She takes care of him, so I don't have to worry about him. I give her money every month toward his support, and visit him sometimes."

Sensing that he wanted to put that part of his life behind him, she didn't inquire any further. Though she didn't care for the idea of the child, she was proud that Richard had been responsible in providing for him.

They married, renovated an old house, had two children, and lived a close and happy life.

Every so often, usually on a Saturday afternoon, Richard would say, "I'm going to see Michael." That was all the conversation they had of him. April refused to dwell on the money that went out of their account every month to the boy's mother.

This peaceful coexistence with the phantom child had come to an abrupt end five days ago. That evening, the telephone rang with a call for Richard. After a short conversation, he hung up.

"Vanessa Hay is dead," he informed her. "She was crossing the street at Sixteenth and Main when she was hit by a truck and killed."

"Who is Vanessa Hay?" asked April. The name was unfamiliar to her.

"She's my former girlfriend—Michael's mother."

"Do you think you should go to the funeral?" April didn't know what else to say; she couldn't offer condolences regarding someone who now meant very little to Richard.

"Yes, I will go." He paused, then looked squarely at her with his intense blue eyes. "This has an implication for our family. We will have to bring Michael here to live with us."

April felt a sense of panic arising in her. "Oh, no!" she exclaimed. "I can't do it. You know me, I'm not comfortable with looking after other people's children. I have enough to do looking after my own."

Richard didn't press the issue. "I'll have to see what else I can do then," he said quietly. "After all, he is my child and my responsibility."

The issue hung between them for the next few days.

———

April's activities with her children were interrupted by the arrival of her mother. Nathan ran to greet her with a squeal of "Gwamma!" and gave her a hug. Anna lifted her chubby arms to be picked up.

After Mother was seated with the children snuggled on her lap, she asked April, "Is Richard at the funeral?"

"Yes, he is," replied April.

"Dad and I met Michael the other day. He was with Richard at the mall. He seems like a nice boy."

"Oh," replied April uneasily. She was still disturbed by her argument with Richard that morning.

"What's the problem?" her mother asked.

"Oh, Mom. I don't like to talk about what goes on between me and Richard, but it seems as if this boy has come between us. We had such a wonderful life, but now Richard wants us to bring the boy to live with us. That will just ruin the life we have."

"I guess there isn't any other alternative."

"Actually, there is," said April. "It's a very good alternative. Richard tried to get foster care for the boy, but they refused. They said he had the means to look after the child himself. He found a boarding school, but it was too expensive. He called different relatives, but either they were unwilling or unable to take the child. The only ones who were interested were Richard's cousin Jay and his wife Leslie. They said they wouldn't foster him, but they wanted to adopt him. I think it's the perfect solution to the problem. It would free Richard from this encumbrance, but he is adamant that he is not giving up his child."

Her mother sat quietly and listened as April continued her rant.

"Mom, I don't like to unload on you like this, but Richard is being so unreasonable. Here is this couple who want the boy and have a good home to offer him. Why is Richard hanging on to him? It isn't as if he and the boy are close; they've seen each other so rarely. Why does he want to keep the child when he would be better off with new adoptive parents?"

Mother sighed deeply. "Poor April. Poor, poor April. You have your home, a caring husband, two wonderful children, no health problems, no major worries. Is a little boy going to be such a hardship in your life?"

April looked surprised. "Mom, I thought you would be on my side. Why should I take on a child who is someone else's responsibility? I kept myself out of trouble when I was young so I wouldn't have a mess to clean up in my life—like some of the other girls. Richard was lucky enough to marry a virgin. I wasn't that lucky. I don't want to pretend to be one big, happy, blended family with this child. I've seen too many people go through that pretence."

He mother shook her head. "Let me explain something to you, dear. Richard is much more attached to his son than you realize. He has been visiting him several times a week for years. He often stops in to see him on his way home from work."

"But he never told me that. I thought it was only once a month—or less!" exclaimed April. "Why did he tell you and Dad this? He never told me."

"Listen, dear. Richard isn't an easy talker at the best of times, but the other day he seemed to need someone to confide in. He wanted to talk about this burden he has been carrying alone. A burden he should have been able to share with you. After all, you are a married couple; you should be sharing the burdens as well as the good times. Remember that part of the marriage vows—for better or for worse."

"But you were okay with the way things were."

"Michael's mother was alive then. She could look after him, and his dad could visit and give him the attention he needed from a father. The situation has changed."

"But I don't even babysit," April said. "And now you think I should become a permanent babysitter to this boy?"

"It's good to have ideals. That's how we raised you. But sometimes the best ideal is kindness. You have a wonderful opportunity to show kindness to a motherless child, to make a home for him. No, I don't think you should be his babysitter; you should be his mother. You should adopt him!"

"What? Adopt this boy? Be a mother to a child who isn't mine?"

As her mother stood and prepared to leave, she made one final comment. "You have carried resentment against Michael ever since you knew of his existence. I don't know why. It isn't the child's fault."

After her mother left, April walked over to the bookshelf and took down her high school yearbook. Her mother's accusation was true—she resented those who got themselves into tough situations and then expected others to help deal with the consequences.

She flipped the pages to her class pictures. Halfway down the page she saw the photo of Tasha Krensky smirking into the camera. She remembered the afternoon Tasha had approached her in the school cafeteria. She had been carrying her baby in his car seat after picking him up from the daycare room. Loser Daycare—that's what April and her friends had called it, a place for loser babies and their loser mothers. It was always the same kind of girls who got knocked up—no life, no brains, no interests, no future.

Tasha had placed the baby's car seat on the table. "Oh, April, I have a favour to ask. Will you watch Ducker for five minutes while I go to the bathroom?"

"Okay, but come right back. I have a class in ten minutes."

After Tasha had gone, April looked at the squirming infant. Ducker! What a stupid name! She had noticed the dirt between his tiny fingers and in the folds of his neck. Didn't Tasha bathe him? Wasn't she smart enough to do that much?

Tasha hadn't returned in five minutes, or in ten minutes. April had carried the baby to the daycare room but found it locked. With no other choice open to her, she had returned to the cafeteria. There she had waited another forty minutes until Tasha showed up, wide-eyed and apologetic.

April had walked into history class a few minutes before the dismissal bell.

The next morning, she had been called into the principal's office to explain her unexcused absence. Half an hour later, still fuming with annoyance, April had seen Tasha in the hallway talking with her friends. She had walked right up to her and exploded. "You got me in trouble yesterday!"

"But I said I was sorry," Tasha had explained sweetly.

"Like you meant it," April had replied. "You're not smart enough to keep out of a boy's bed, and not smart enough to keep from having a baby. Then you think it's okay to dump him in someone else's lap. Then you say you're sorry!"

Tasha had sneered at her. "You're just jealous because the boys like me instead of you."

"Listen, sweetie! The kind of guys you attract, I can do without. Someday I'm going to have a good husband and babies, in that order." After this parting shot, April had stalked away. She then turned to add an extra remark: "If you ever dump your kid in my lap again, I'm going to throw him out in the snow."

That evening she had sobbed out her frustration to her mother.

"That stupid girl and her stupid baby, they got me in trouble!"

"It's not the child's fault," her mother had said quietly.

———

With her mother's remark ringing in her ears, April closed the yearbook and placed it back on the shelf. She thought of Richard and the one major error of his life. It was better that his child go to a new home, where he would be a welcome addition to the family—instead of a mistake. The boy would adjust, and Richard would get over it.

Late in the afternoon, April began her preparations for dinner. Richard hadn't returned from the funeral yet. She fed the children and put them to bed, but still there was no sign of him.

As the evening progressed, April started to feel anxious. Where was Richard? He had planned to be home around five o'clock. Was he all right? Had anything happened to him?

Around nine o'clock, the phone rang. She raced to answer it.

It was Richard's cousin, Jay. After she explained that Richard hadn't come home, Jay said, "Tell him that Michael is very upset. He cried until he made himself sick. Leslie and I don't know what to do with him."

April was surprised. "I didn't know he was at your place."

"Richard brought him here this afternoon and said we could adopt him," explained Jay. "We'd like to have him, but I don't think it's going to work out. He's grieving for his mother—and for his father, too. Will you ask Richard to call me?"

"Of course," she said, then she hung up the phone.

Where was Richard? What had happened to him? Dependable, predictable Richard had disappeared for several hours without telling anyone. According to her mother, he also hadn't told her about all his visits to his son. She realized suddenly that there was a gap between them, and it was wider than she had ever known.

An hour later, April heard the car pull into the yard.

A minute later, Richard opened the door and walked in. He looked tired and pale, and his eyes were grief-stricken.

April ran to him and put her arms around him. "I was so worried about you," she said with relief.

They sat down on the couch together, with April holding his hand.

"I took Michael to Jay and Leslie. I've been driving for the last four hours, trying to get used to the idea of giving away my child. It was the hardest thing I had ever done," he explained, his voice breaking. "I hope you can understand that it was just as hard as it would be to give away Nathan or Anna."

April silently put her thoughts together. Richard had been leading a double life so that she didn't have to, so that his son didn't have to. He was willing to endure heartbreak for her so that she could be comfortable in her own family. In those few minutes she accepted what she, in spite of her protests, had always known to be the only acceptable course of action.

She took her husband's face in her hands and looked into his eyes. "Tell Jay and Leslie that they can't have him," she said. "If anyone is going to adopt Michael, it's going to be me."

———◆———

The next morning, April waited nervously. She ran to the window from time to time, watching for the arrival of Richard and Michael. Although she had decided to take Michael into the family and be a mother to him, she was still uncomfortable. Suppose he was difficult or angry.

Suppose he was defiant to her. Suppose she couldn't manage him. Suppose she couldn't love him.

Then she saw the car pull into the driveway. As they walked toward the house, she noticed Michael's resemblance to Richard, the same intense eyes, the same mouth, the same chin.

She opened the door and looked at the boy. Nathan raced to give his new brother a hug.

April reached out her hand and laid it on Michael's shoulder. "Welcome to your new home," she said.

9.

THE VALEDICTORY

CARA SORENSEN PINNED A CORSAGE ON HER MIDNIGHT BLUE gown. She felt attractive with her new hairdo, sweet face, and slight figure, a young girl on the threshold of adulthood.

"I'm almost ready," she said to her father's reflection in the mirror. "Couldn't you wait somewhere else?"

Her mother's voice echoed from the hall. "Ted, come down here. You'll not hurry her up by hanging around the doorway."

Ted crossed the room to give Cara a quick hug.

"I can't believe you're finished high school, and with such a high academic record. And so grown up, too! You are smart *and* beautiful."

"Da–ad!" Despite the compliments, Cara's head still ached and the knots in her stomach tightened. She'd been told many times that she was pretty and slim like her mother, but what did all that matter right now?

"I'd think you'd be happy today," her father added. "I can tell something's wrong. You've not been yourself for a while. What is it? Give your old dad a clue."

"Not now, Dad, okay?" She attempted a smile. "I can handle it. Thanks anyway."

"Well, all right, my lovely yearbook editor, scholarship winner, valedictorian," he said as he left her. "Wave to me and your mom."

Glad to be alone for a few moments, Cara smoothed a stray curl behind her ear, took a deep breath, and picked up her clutch purse. Her speech was in there, folded neatly, waiting.

When Cara and her parents arrived at the school cafeteria, they found the place transformed into a banquet room fit for the important occasion. Blue and gold streamers adorned the ceiling. Centrepieces featuring mini-grad hats sat on the tables. Cara glanced around at the equally transformed students and teachers. Suits and elegant dresses had replaced the usual jeans and sweats.

She noticed Treva Rutledge across the room, and groaned. *Why did she even come to the grad? She didn't pass all her courses. She isn't even graduating.*

Cara swallowed hard as Treva made her way through the crowd towards a group of classmates that included Rob Terloni. No wonder all the guys were staring. In her tight, low-cut black dress, Treva looked and walked like she belonged on a New York runway, not some small town grad. Her wavy shoulder-length auburn hair shimmered beneath the lights, and she'd obviously given a lot of time to her make-up.

But Rob didn't seem impressed. He sauntered over to Cara, a glass of punch in his hand. He looked smart in his suit and tie.

As Rob opened his mouth to speak, he lurched forward and dropped the glass. It shattered on the gymnasium floor and sent sticky yellow punch onto Rob's new shoes.

A penitent Treva stood beside him. "I'm so sorry," she exclaimed. "I didn't mean to bump into you. It was an accident. Honest."

Just like all your other accidents, thought Cara as she rolled her eyes toward the ceiling.

Rob, however, chose to smooth over the situation. "No harm done, Treva. It's okay." He wiped his shoes with a napkin. "Did she do that on purpose?" he asked, after Treva had gone.

"I didn't see, but I wouldn't be surprised if she did," replied Cara.

At dinner, Rob and his family sat opposite the Sorensens. Cara was glad; Rob was the only friend she had left, the only one who understood. They filled their plates with salads, roast beef, vegetables, and biscuits from the buffet, then returned to the table to enjoy their dinner, along with the pleasant conversation that accompanied it.

As the satisfied crowd started to mingle, Treva came to Cara's side. "I brought you dessert," she said with a sweet smile. "We haven't always been on good terms, but I really want to be friends."

"That's very kind of you," replied Cara without smiling. She remembered the trashing of the yearbook files and Treva's amusement over it.

As Treva walked away, Rob quickly exchanged his strawberry shortcake for Cara's. "I saw her pull a can from her purse and spray it on the dessert. Let her think she got away with her trick."

Cara nodded, but as she toyed with her whipped cream, an idea formed in her mind. *I'm finished with this school. I have good references and no one here can do anything to hurt me again. Why not say something? No one listens when I speak, but I can write well—and I can read what I write. This time they'll have to listen; they can't brush me aside.*

She pulled her valedictory address out of her purse— the sentimental, useless, forgettable speech that had won the approval of Mr. Selesky, the teacher in charge of the graduation ceremony.

"I have to go and brush up my speech," she told her parents. "I'll see you later."

She found Mr. Selesky in the crowd.

"Will you let me into the computer room?" she asked. "I need to make some last-minute changes to my valedictory."

"Your speech is fine," he said. "Do you really need to be so particular?"

"I'd really like to make a few changes."

Reluctantly he unlocked the door to the computer room.

Seated at the computer, Cara opened the valedictory file and began to edit her composition. *First paragraph—good. Second paragraph—delete and add new material.*

A half-hour later, she gathered her sheets of paper from the printer, folded them, and went out to join her classmates.

From the front row of the auditorium, Cara had a good view of the stage, where several of the teachers were seated. She was glad she wouldn't have to look at Mr. Selesky or the principal, Mr. Fife, while she spoke.

After the presentation of diplomas and the awarding of scholarships, Mr. Fife introduced Cara as the valedictorian. She rose, walked up the steps to the podium, and nervously unfolded her papers.

With a slight tremor in her voice, she began. "Teachers, students, ladies and gentlemen, this ceremony brings us to the end of a journey that started four years ago. At that time we looked forward to new challenges in our classes and our activities. It was a step up from the years at middle school. At this time I would like to express the thanks of the graduating class to the teachers who worked so tirelessly to help us in our efforts. Without you, we would not have reached this point in our lives."

Cara paused and drew a deep breath before continuing. "Ladies and gentlemen, I would like to claim that it was all good, but that wouldn't be true. Some of it was bad, and sometimes the bad seemed to overwhelm the good. I am going to be honest and straightforward about it, because we students, teachers, and parents need to face up to a serious problem and deal with it, instead of just tiptoeing around it. The problem is bullying."

She stood straight at the microphone, her voice firm and strong. "When I came here in Grade Nine, I was warned by other students not to go into the north wing, because I might get jumped. I was also advised that it wasn't safe to go up or down the staircases alone. I found out why on the day a fight broke out on the stairs between two boys. Were the staff members even aware that these were unsafe places in the school?"

Cara stopped as Mr. Selesky approached and stood beside her. "This isn't the speech you prepared. Give your original speech, please."

Cara looked him straight in the eye. "This has to be said now—or I will email a copy to all the students later."

A few voices called from the audience, "Let her continue."

Mr. Selesky nodded and returned to his seat.

"Do you remember when Mandy Villiers was beaten and kicked by three other girls?" she continued. "She had to be sent to the hospital, and the police were called. Those girls were given a three-day suspension. After the three days were over, they came back to school laughing about their *vacation*. What kind of punishment was that?

"Many other instances occurred—tripping, punching, verbal abuse, teasing, name-calling, putdowns. Sometimes a self-appointed cool person would round up a group to torment someone he or she considered uncool.

"For example, one day Rachel Foster was in the girls locker room changing after gym class. One of the other girls took a photo of her, partly naked, and posted it to all her Facebook contacts. They had a big laugh over it, but Rachel was devastated. She left school soon after that, because she suffered from anxiety. The day before she left, she said to me, 'School isn't about education anymore; it's about survival.'

"Since I've always been interested in writing, I worked on the newsletter and the yearbook committees. I decided to write an article for the newsletter describing bullying in the school. I submitted it, only to be told that the newsletter was intended to report on extracurricular activities, and that bullying was a problem for the staff to handle. I can't agree. It's a student problem, too—especially a student problem.

"I might have been able to lay low and avoid the bullying scene, except for the fact that Treva Rutledge took a dislike to me." The audience gasped as Cara openly named one of the bullies. "Yes, she seemed to dislike and harass many other girls—all of whom were smaller than she was. If she was reported, she turned on the charm—and the tears, and claimed that everyone was out to get her. I reported her and was asked why I was trying to get the girl in trouble."

Cara hesitated at the memory of her father's words: *"I'm sure you're exaggerating. You shouldn't be so sensitive."*

"Then someone vandalized the yearbook records, and the committee had to start over again. Nothing was ever proven, but Treva treated it like a good joke," Cara said. "Another day, when I was walking down the hall carrying an armful of books and papers, she tripped me and shoved me onto the floor. It took several minutes of dodging her before I could pick up all my stuff. She really enjoyed the cat and mouse game."

Cara shivered before carrying on with the ugliest memory of her school years. "Then there was an incident that almost made me quit school. One day I was in the washroom, when Treva walked in. She carried a bag in one hand, and with the other she scooped out some smelly stuff and smeared it all over my clothes, hair, and face. It turned out to be a mixture of mud and poop. I have never felt so humiliated in my life!" Cara fought to control her tears. Having regained her composure, she continued. "I ran outside and threw up a couple of times. Then I ran all the way home. I couldn't get on the bus looking and smelling like that. Fortunately no one was home, so I stuffed my dirty clothes in a garbage bag and hid it in my closet. After that I took a good long shower. I made a mistake doing this. I should have gone to Mr. Fife or called my parents to come, but it was just too humiliating. I thought of some nasty tricks I could play on Treva, but why get myself into trouble over her?"

Cara saw the audience shifting uncomfortably. It was time to wrap it up.

"This is a strange goodbye to high school, but I had to deliver this message. It's time to do something constructive here, time to hand out real consequences for such behaviour. It's time to enforce rules. Yes, I know we all wore pink t-shirts on anti-bullying day, but unless each and every case is taken seriously, and handled as it should be, the whole anti-bullying campaign is just hypocrisy. I have decided that I will never again remain silent in the face of injustice. If people won't listen when I speak, I will write it."

Cara folded her paper and walked off the stage. Rob gave her a thumbs-up sign.

"Way to go!" a few graduates exclaimed amid the resounding applause. "That's telling them!"

Mr. Fife spoke into the microphone. "School isn't over yet," he said. "Will the graduating class please remain in your seats? I want to ask you some questions. Cara Sorensen and Treva Rutledge, I want to see you and your parents in my office in ten minutes."

———

On the drive home, the Sorensens discussed the events of the evening.

"I'm proud of you, dear," said Cara's mother. "You were calm and dignified as you answered Mr. Fife's questions. Treva was just sulky and childish."

"I saw you in a new light," remarked Ted. "You've really grown up."

"Thanks," replied Cara. "Somehow graduating doesn't seem to matter as much as becoming more mature."

"You're right about that. There will be many more challenges ahead of you, and you will need maturity to handle them all," said Ted as he smiled at his grown-up daughter.

10.

FAMILY TREASURE

"No, I can't possibly go to England with you," Janet spoke into the phone.

"But, Mom," pleaded Laurel, "you never go anywhere. I know you don't want to travel alone, but this time you would have us with you."

"It still isn't possible. I have enough money to live on, but not enough to spend on travel. If I spend it all now, I will face a penniless old age."

"Don't you save Air Miles?" asked Laurel.

"Honey, the number of Air Miles I have saved would buy me a ticket from Winnipeg to Regina; it wouldn't get me to England," Janet said. "But thanks for asking. I'm glad you and Bryan still want me around."

"Of course we do, and the kids would love to have you. But I understand about the cost."

After her conversation with Laurel, Janet returned her brother's call.

"Hello, George. How are you?" she asked.

"I'm fine, thank you," George said. "Did you read the closing stock market quotations?"

"George, you should know by this time that I never read the financial pages. I don't even understand them."

He ignored her remark. "Metals are high. Silver is selling for seventy cents a gram, gold for seventy-five."

Janet sighed. George should have been a stockbroker instead of an electronics dealer. He never thought of anything but investments.

She changed the subject. "Have you been to see Mom this week?"

"Yes, I went to see her on Thursday evening. She showed me the watercolour paintings she did. I'm glad she's so well taken care of at the seniors' lodge." George quickly returned to his former topic. "There's a reason I wanted to tell you about metals. It is because of Keith Widget."

"Oh, yes," she replied vaguely. She hadn't seen George's friend in several years. "How is he doing?"

"Not well at all. He has had two surgeries for a brain tumour. About fifteen years ago, he and I made a bet. The loser would give the winner a silver bar. I won the bet, and Keith gave me the silver. I have kept it all this time. I discussed it with Sharon, and we've decided to sell the bar and give the money to Keith. He's on disability insurance and could use a little help."

"That's very kind of you and Sharon," Janet said. "Where would you go to sell the silver? Is there anyone reliable who deals in it? Someone who wouldn't rip you off?"

"Yes, Southgate Coin on Cumberland Avenue. They have a reputation as honest dealers. They buy old coins as well as silver dishes and utensils. They melt them down and sell the silver to the mint."

"I see." Janet was rather bored by George's constant focus on money. Still, it was generous of him to give the money from the silver bar to Keith.

"Another thing, Jan. Didn't Mom have a china bowl with blue trim around the edge? Is it still around?"

"Maybe. I have most of Mom's old dishes here."

"China with blue trim is very popular now. You could advertise it on the internet and probably get about two hundred dollars for it."

"Maybe I'll look for it. Thanks for the advice. And say hello to Keith for me."

After she hung up the phone, Janet walked into the kitchen. She opened the cupboard and searched the top shelf, where she kept her unused dishes. She took out the bowl George had mentioned. It was cream-coloured with midnight-blue edging, intertwined with an intricate gold design.

Two hundred dollars isn't much nowadays, she thought. *I would rather keep the bowl.*

She placed it on the centre of her dining table, where she could admire it.

She looked at the two crystal vases on top of the bookcase. They had also belonged to Mother. The bone china tea set was displayed in the corner cabinet. Knowing how much Janet admired it, her mother had given it to her as a wedding gift.

The next day, Janet descended to the basement to search through the boxes of her mother's former possessions. She had brought them to her home when her mother had moved to the senior's lodge. Delicate china and fragile stemware, many of them were relics of a bygone era. Who used such things nowadays? It was easier to use kitchen dishes and coffee mugs for guests instead of delicate articles that she wouldn't put in the dishwasher.

"I may not keep them all," Janet had told her mother. "I want a few of them as mementos of you, but I don't want my home to look like an antique museum."

"I understand," her mother had replied. "And Sharon definitely won't want any of them."

As Janet looked through the box, memories filled her thoughts. She set aside several cheap ornaments for the next garage sale. She admired the teapot that had belonged to her grandmother, the lace tablecloth that her aunt had made, a silver cream and sugar set. Then, at the bottom of the box, she saw the wooden chest containing sterling silver cutlery. It had sat on the sideboard since her childhood. She opened it and remembered.

—◆—

When George and Sharon had married, Mother had planned it as a special gift for them.

"I plan to give them the set of silverware. What do you think?" she had asked Janet.

"It's yours to give," Janet had replied. "You gave me your tea set for a wedding gift. I think it's a good idea to give the silverware to George and Sharon."

"I saved coupons for years to get most of it."

"Yes, I know that."

"Then Mother and Father bought me the rest of the set."

Janet had never known where the coupons originated. Had they been an advertising giveaway from some company?

Nowadays we have travel points, she thought. *Maybe in those days they had coupons.*

Sharon had smiled when her mother-in-law presented her with the chest of silverware.

"It's beautiful," Sharon had said warmly. "It will be lovely to use it when we have guests for dinner. Thank you so much."

A few days later, when Janet was visiting her mother, Sharon had suddenly arrived at the front door, carrying the wooden chest. She'd walked into the house, placed the chest of silver on the table, and said angrily, "George told me this is a used set. He also told me you got it by saving coupons. How could you give us something old and cheap like this?" She had walked out, leaving her mother-in-law with a hurt that was never completely forgotten. The next day, Mother had delivered her a replacement wedding gift: a set of bath towels.

———

Two days later, Janet acted on the resolve slowly growing inside her. She took a cardboard box and placed in it the wooden chest containing the silver, the cream and sugar set, and a silver tray that had been a gift to her and Allan on their twenty-fifth wedding anniversary.

She drove the length of the avenue with the address clearly in mind—1468 Cumberland. Her confidence was at a low point as she entered the front door of Southgate Coin, carrying her precious box of family treasure.

I don't know for sure if any of this is real silver, she thought. *George would know, but I'm not going to ask him. Maybe I'm just making a laughing stock of myself.*

She put on a polite manner as she addressed the young man at the counter. "Please tell me if this stuff has any value. If it has, would you be interested in purchasing it?"

The young man picked up and examined each item, his manner business-like. He showed no sign of the amusement Janet had feared.

He placed the cream and sugar back in the box, but the rest he carefully weighed. "That's 3,896 grams at seventy cents a gram," he said, punching the numbers into the calculator. "That comes to $2,727.20. Since it's a large amount, I'll have to get the manager to verify it."

Janet's calm demeanour masked her excitement as a short middle-aged woman examined the silverware and tray, then rechecked the calculations.

After leaving Southgate Coin with her empty wooden chest, cream and sugar set, and cheque for $2,727.20, Janet permitted herself a squeal of delight. "Yes!"

Grinning widely, she thought, *Eat your heart out, Sharon. This could have been yours.*

Back home she quickly phoned Laurel. "Guess what?" she said. "I'm going to England with you."

11.

EMERGENCY!

DR. MEL SPENCER WALKED INTO THE STAFF LOUNGE adjacent to the emergency room of the city hospital. It had been a busy day. Of course, it was always busy in the ER, and always unpredictable, but Saturdays seemed worse. Fortunately, the adrenalin rush of emergency care suited the doctor perfectly. Seeing patients in an office was dull by comparison; he was glad to work in the ER. He was one of the lucky ones, with a job that was always stimulating.

He poured himself a cup of coffee, then dialled his home phone number.

"Hello, sweetheart," he said as soon as Tracy answered. "How are you?"

"I'm fine. How are you?"

"I'm tired! It's been a hectic day. I'll be glad to get home and relax."

"I just talked to Jeff and Laura this morning. They would like us to go out to dinner with them. I suggested we meet them at seven."

"No way, honey. I'm worn out. I just want to take it easy."

"You'll have three hours to rest before we go out. That's plenty of time."

"It's not enough. When I get home after a workday, I just want to stay there."

"Why do we have to stay home all the time because you're tired?" Tracy replied angrily. "Do I always have to put my social activities on hold because you're spending your life either working or sleeping?"

"Why don't you go out yourself, without me?"

"And be a third wheel? You know very well that a woman isn't welcome at events without her man. I'll just have to tell them we can't make it. See you later, and we'll have a boring evening together."

Mel hung up the phone with annoyance. Why were women always so keen on running to visits and parties, or inviting guests over? Couldn't they just stay home? Didn't Tracy appreciate the work he did, how important it was? Didn't she realize how exhausted he was after a day's work?

He had just taken a sip of coffee when his pager announced, "Dr. Spencer to ER!"

He put down his cup and hurried to emergency.

A nurse handed him a chart. "The patient is on her way by ambulance," she said.

The doctor quickly read the chart. Sarah Beneton, female, aged sixteen, overdosed on pills.

The ambulance shrieked into the driveway and the attendants wheeled in the patient on a stretcher. One of them handed the doctor the prescription bottle that had been the source of the overdose pills. He read it quickly. Prescription medication usually indicated a suicide attempt.

He noticed the girl's delicate frame and sweet face. She reminded him of his daughter Kristen. Would it be this way for her some day? Kristen, at fourteen, seemed to be angry all the time, yelling at him, taking out her frustrations on her mother. Sarah Beneton hadn't succeeded in ending her life. Would Kristen? Why was he even thinking it?

When the patient was stable, the doctor headed for the waiting room.

"Are the parents of Sarah Beneton here?" he asked.

A pale woman with anxiety written over her features answered, "I'm Sarah's mother."

"Hello, I'm Dr. Spencer."

"Is Sarah going to be all right?"

"Sarah is out of danger now. We will keep her here overnight for observation. You can see her in a few minutes. Then I'd like to talk to you about referring her for a psychiatric assessment. It really is necessary that she see a specialist."

Mrs. Beneton's eyes filled with tears. "Oh yes, please, we need all the help we can get. I don't know what to do with her anymore. She's so unhappy."

As the doctor returned to his patient, he reflected that middle-aged and elderly patients were brought to the ER with heart attacks and strokes; young people came with drug and alcohol overdoses, suicide attempts, and automobile accidents. Why did it have to be this way? Why were the young people throwing their lives away on stupidity?

His own life had never been that way. Some of his classmates had drunk alcohol; he knew that. Mom and Dad had made it clear that wasn't an option.

"You say you want to go to medical school and become a doctor. You are not going to do it on booze, drugs, fast cars, or fast women," Dad had advised. "Keep away from that stuff, or they'll just steal medical school away from you."

He had followed their advice, with one recent exception—the woman.

Dad had disapproved completely. "Mel, she will cost you. She'll cost you money, and she'll cost you heartache—yours and other people's."

These thoughts ran through Mel's mind as he approached his young patient and sat down.

"Were you trying to kill yourself?" he asked quietly.

She nodded.

"What is so awful that you want to end your life?"

"My dad hates me," she said angrily.

"Parents usually love their children very much. Why do you think your father hates you?"

"Because he acts hateful. He hates my mother and he hates me. He left us for another woman. He wouldn't have done that if he didn't hate us." She burst into tears and began sobbing. "Mom was so heartbroken. She cried every day. She still does." She paused to swallow a few more sobs. "I used to think my dad was the best. You can't imagine how it hurts to know your father is just a jerk. It feels like he stabbed us in the heart, and we have to move to an apartment because we can't afford a house, while he's moving his girlfriend—and her children—into a beautiful new house. He says he loves me, but he really hates me. So I'm going to hate him, too. If I died, maybe he would feel rotten about it."

While she'd been speaking, the doctor had been thinking. *There's nothing more I can do for her state of mind. I'll refer her to Dr. Idello. She'll get the treatment she needs from him.*

He couldn't do anything more for this patient, yet in the recesses of his memory he heard Kristen's voice: "Dad, I hate you!" When Tracy had tried to intervene, Kristen had slapped her.

In the waiting room, he found Sarah's mother looking more composed. A man was sitting beside her.

"This is Sarah's father," she said.

"Hello, I'm Dr. Spencer." He turned to Mrs. Beneton. "Would you like to see Sarah for a few minutes? She's down the hall, second door on the right."

That's when Mel realized he wasn't finished with this patient after all. He made an instant decision—for Sarah, and also for Kristen.

"Mr. Beneton, let's go into the office," he said. "We can talk privately there."

When they were seated, Mel began.

"I want to get right to the point. Sarah will recover physically, but a suicide attempt is a cry for help. She should receive psychiatric evaluation. I'm referring her to Dr. Idello, who is well experienced in his field. His office will get in touch with you."

"Thank you, Doctor," the father said.

Mel took a deep breath, thought of Sarah and Kristen, and so many others like them. Then he plunged ahead. "Dr. Idello will be able to help Sarah cope with her current problems, but in the long run he will not be able to remove the sense of betrayal she feels. She tells me you have separated from her mother."

"Yes, that's true. But is it really any of your concern?"

"Anything that affects my patient's health concerns me. The point is that there are too many youngsters like Sarah. Their parents are more concerned about their own happiness and pleasure than about their children's needs." Mel paused before taking the next step. "Mr. Beneton, would you seriously consider returning to your wife and family? If you did that, and asked their forgiveness, you would help Sarah far more than the medical profession ever could."

Sarah's father looked solemn. "I don't really think I can do that."

"Please, think about it. Is it really fair that you have acquired your own happiness by plunging your family into misery?" Mel was surprised at his own eloquence.

"I'm still not sure it's possible to go back to them."

"Please think about it—for Sarah's sake."

After Mr. Beneton left the office, Mel logged onto his iPad. He typed his wife's email address and began composing a letter.

Dear Gwyneth,

I am writing to ask if you would be willing to take me back as your husband. I was wrong to leave you, and I know I hurt both you and Kristen very badly. Please forgive me, and give us a chance to start over.

If you cannot find it in your heart to take me back for yourself, will you do it for Kristen? She has been very hurt. She's still so young and shouldn't have to live with our separation.

If you will take me back, I promise that I will work with you to make a stable, happy marriage. I also promise that Tracy will be out of my life, and there will never again be anyone like her. I did a bad job of keeping the promises I made the day we were married, but I will keep these promises I am making now.

Please email or phone soon.

—Mel

12.

FIRST BOYFRIEND

Julie sat quietly in the living room of her home one evening, tired after a day of doing her job and her household chores. The work never seemed to end for a widow with a teenaged daughter. In all the bereavement literature, why did no one ever mention that the responsibilities two people used to handle now had to be handled by one person? No one ever thought of that; they wrote of her grief, her tears, of helping her daughter through her grief, but they never mentioned that the workload doubled. The weight of responsibility seemed unbearable.

She glanced with annoyance toward the front hall, where her daughter Emma had left her gym bag. Her sweat clothes were thrown untidily across it, her shoes and socks scattered across the carpet.

How opposite she and her daughter were! She was tidy; Emma was messy. She was organized; Emma was casual. She did her work promptly; Emma procrastinated.

Through the window, Julie noticed Nancy walk up the sidewalk. She sighed. After a tiring day, she was in no mood to deal with Nancy.

She opened the door and greeted her guest with as much courtesy as her tired brain could muster. "How are you this evening?" Julie asked.

"I'm fine, thank you," replied Nancy crisply as she sat down on the couch. She looked inquisitively around the room. "Where's Emma?"

"She's at Carla Jackson's. A few of the girls are doing schoolwork together."

"Wouldn't she accomplish more if she studied at home alone?" demanded Nancy in an authoritative tone. "I don't let Taryn do schoolwork with her friends. They're more likely to goof off."

"Emma has to take responsibility for her own studies. I have enough of my own work to deal with."

"But what if she fails a course because she hasn't had adequate supervision?"

"If she fails a course, she will simply have to do it over again. Hopefully she'll learn from the experience." Julie wondered how a young girl was supposed to grow up and make decisions in the real world if she wasn't allowed to practice decision-making while in school.

Nancy turned her attention to another topic. "I hear that Emma is dating Jeff Sanders!"

"Oh, they've gone out together twice," said Julie in an unconcerned tone. "It's nothing to get excited about." She wished Nancy would give up the habit of making mountains out of molehills.

"I thought you would be very excited! After all, this is her first boyfriend. I was concerned she might feel left out of the dating scene, especially since Taryn is very popular with the boys."

Julie sighed again. "I don't think Emma is worried about popularity," she replied, thinking of her daughter's placid temperament. The two of them would probably laugh over Nancy's excesses later.

"Of course, you're going to provide her with birth control," Nancy stated. "It's important that a girl have protection."

Julie sat upright, stunned by this suggestion. She paused before answering, then turned deliberately to Nancy and said with emphasis, "It takes every penny to put food on the table and pay the bills. Where am I supposed to find the money to buy birth control so that some irresponsible brat can rip off my daughter's body free of charge?"

Nancy was not deterred. "But it's very important to protect her. You know the pressures on young people nowadays. If you need help financially, Public Health would supply the birth control."

"That's the kind of help I don't need," replied Julie shortly.

"But what if she got pregnant? You really should consider birth control."

"The kind of birth control Emma can use is to stay out of the boy's bed. If she gets pregnant, she'll have to take responsibility for it herself—either give up the child for adoption or move out of the house and raise it on her own."

"How could you be so cruel?"

"I'm not being cruel, I'm being practical. As I said before, it takes every penny—and, I might add, all my energy. There is no money for birth control, and no energy to look after a baby."

"Well, I still think you're being impractical, Julie." Nancy gathered up her jacket and prepared to leave.

After Nancy had gone, Julie indulged in a few tears. She could manage her own life, but she had a hard time managing people who wanted to manage her. How she missed Dave. If he was still here, the Nancys of the world wouldn't be riding her back.

Around ten o'clock, Emma arrived home. She tossed her books on the table and sprawled on the couch with a contented sigh. "I got all my science homework caught up. Carla was a big help. She's so smart at explaining things."

"That's good, dear. I'm glad it was worthwhile," Julie said. "What about the dishes? I expected you to do them."

"I said I'd do them this evening, and I will." Emma headed toward the kitchen. "I just didn't say what time."

As Emma started filling the sink with water, Julie followed her into the kitchen. "Nancy was here this evening."

Emma chuckled. "What was she fussing about this time?"

Julie smiled with amusement. "About you. Number one, your group study session at Carla's. Number two, the fact that you've been going out with Jeff." She refrained from mentioning birth control. It disturbed her more than she cared to discuss with her daughter.

"She should mind her own business," replied Emma. "Why are you friends with her, Mom?"

"She's not really my friend. She's just a hanger-on. Did you notice I don't call her or go to her house?"

Emma nodded. "She never bothered with you when Dad was alive. Why now?"

"Because she thinks I'm a poor helpless widow who needs her? She's probably telling herself what a kind person she is, coming over here to straighten me out."

"She's really just a burden." Emma paused. "Mom, I'm glad you're not like her."

The next day at work, Julie's thoughts returned to her conversation with Nancy. Perhaps she should discuss it with one of the other women. The network of mothers had often been a source of help and encouragement—real encouragement, not interference.

She sat down across from Karen at coffee break and was about to open the topic of birth control when Karen stated, "We took Lara to the hospital yesterday. She is anorexic."

"Oh, how awful," Julie exclaimed. "Will they be able to help her?"

"The doctor will keep her in the hospital for a few days to build up her strength. Then she will need to see a counsellor."

Lynne walked into the room in time to hear Karen's last remark. She pulled up a chair, sat down beside her, and joined the conversation. "A good counsellor could help her a lot. When our Shawna was suffering from depression, the medication helped, but working through issues with a depression counsellor really made all the difference. Don't make the mistake of thinking you should handle it all yourselves."

"Thanks," said Karen. "It really helps to talk things over with you girls."

Julie reflected that she had said or done nothing helpful during the whole conversation.

———

At home on Saturday morning, Julie was in the middle of washing clothes when Emma, clad in her nightgown and housecoat, sauntered into the laundry room.

"I expected you to help me with the laundry this morning," Julie said crossly.

"Sorry, Mom. I slept in. I needed the extra sleep."

"I need the extra sleep, too, but I don't often get it." She drew a deep breath to calm herself. She realized from past experience that arguing with Emma accomplished nothing. She continued to work in silence.

She walked into the kitchen, where Emma was pouring herself a bowl of cereal.

"I have an idea," Julie said. "From now on, suppose you launder your own clothes and bedsheets, instead of us trying to do them together and getting into an argument over it."

"That's fine with me, Mom. But do I have to do them every Saturday morning like you do? Or can I do them whenever I want?"

"Whenever you want. Your clothes are your responsibility. I won't interfere. Just don't leave them scattered over the laundry room floor."

She sat down at the table while Emma ate her breakfast.

"That's a smart idea, Mom," said Emma. "We are never on the same wavelength when it comes to doing house chores. So I'll take care of my own laundry, and you take care of yours."

"Good. I'm glad you agree."

Emma stacked her dishes beside the sink. "Jeff wants to come over this evening. Is that okay with you?"

"Yes, of course," replied Julie. She thought Emma sounded uneasy when she made her request.

That evening, Emma showed Jeff into the living room. She flopped into an easy chair while Jeff seated himself comfortably on the couch. When Julie entered, he stood up and shook her hand. He greeted her politely and she returned his greeting. He was an attractive young man with a courteous manner.

They all sat and engaged in small talk for a few minutes. Emma fidgeted nervously. Why? Emma was never nervous.

The phone rang and Julie stepped out to the hallway to answer it. Karen's voice greeted her. "I really wanted to talk to you yesterday, Julie. You are always so calm, no matter what happens. How do you do it?"

"I'm not always as calm as I look," replied Julie, thinking of the low school grades and the messy bedroom.

Karen started to sob. "We're so worried about Lara. She just isn't the same girl she used to be. What should we do?"

Julie paused before replying. "Karen, I can offer sympathy, but I can't help you. You need the help of professionals. Please get that help for your family." She thought of her meetings with Emma's teachers. She had to admit that while some of them were helpful, others were merely critical. "And don't stop looking until you find the right one who can help you."

As Julie finished the call, she picked up snatches of conversation from the living room.

"Why not?"

"I just don't want to."

"Why don't you want to?"

"No reason."

"Ask your mother."

"No. Don't want to."

"But you owe me."

Julie walked into the room at this juncture. "What does she owe you?" she inquired.

Jeff looked at her with confidence. "When a girl goes out with a boy, she owes him sex," he stated bluntly. "She should get birth control."

A surge of anger arose in Julie, but she kept her voice calm. "Why do you think you have any right to her body?"

"Because I paid for her movie ticket, and paid for her hamburger and milkshake," he replied in a matter-of-fact tone.

Julie decided the time to contain her anger had passed. She glared at the young man. "Just who do you think you are? What makes you think that a girl's body can be bought for the price of a movie or a milkshake?"

Jeff looked shaken. He sputtered apologetically, "I'm sorry—I meant—she needs protection."

"You think I have money to throw around so you can get serviced at Emma's expense? I'm not going to stand for this nonsense, and I'll tell you why. It's because I love my daughter. She is more precious to me than anything, definitely too precious for your lowlife intentions." Having finished her rant, she added, "I've heard enough of this stupidity. You are no longer welcome in my home. You may leave."

Emma was silent during her mother's outburst. She watched as her mother opened the front door. Jeff walked out with sagging shoulders, his assurance deflated.

Julie sighed as she closed the door. Her anger was spent. She considered her daughter and the disappointing departure of her first boyfriend.

"I guess I ruined things for you with your boyfriend," she said sympathetically. "But I couldn't go along with that."

Emma ran across the room and threw her arms around her mother's neck. "Thanks for sticking up for me, Mom. I really didn't want to sleep with him. He was selfish—and stupid."

Julie heaved a sigh of relief as she returned her daughter's hug.

"Mom, I want you to know that I'm not like those girls who think they're going to marry Mr. Right by sleeping with several Mr. Wrongs first."

As Emma's arms loosened, Julie's viewpoint shifted dramatically. Lynne's daughter suffered from depression, Karen's daughter from anorexia, and Taryn gained her popularity by sleeping with boys. What were her worries in comparison? A messy room and a tendency to procrastinate?

"I'm so glad I have a daughter like you," she said tenderly. "You're the best."

13.

THE MAN WITH THE BIRDS

Joy picked up her purse and keys as she glanced at her husband. As usual, Mark was lounging in his easy chair with a book open on his lap, a stack of books and magazines on the table beside him, and the remote control within easy reach.

Mark's couch potato lifestyle irritated Joy. All he did was go to work and come home to his comfortable chair.

"I'm going to Evergreen Park to take a walk," she said.

"Okay. Is Erin going with you?"

"No, she isn't. Now that the snow has melted and we can't cross-country ski, she's not interested. She likes skiing, not hiking."

"I see," Mark said. "Aren't you going to wear the hiking boots I bought you?"

Joy shook her head "Actually those boots are harder to walk in than track shoes."

"I thought you'd like them," said Mark in a disappointed tone.

Joy headed out the door. On the way to the car, she waved to her neighbour, Ellen.

"Oh, Joy," Ellen called. "Since you're going out, could you pick up my prescription at the drug store?"

Joy groaned. "I won't have time. Better get it delivered."

I'm through with being your gofer, she thought as she hopped into the car.

On the drive to Evergreen Park, Joy experienced yet more frustration. Mark and his misguided generosity— why buy an expensive pair of boots when a medium-priced pair of track shoes worked better? He saw himself as a virtuous husband and father, but really he was clueless. He had no understanding of the constant loneliness in her life, how every activity she did was for the purpose of filling that void: her part-time job, her involvement in the environmental program, her contacts at her children's soccer games and school events, even her hiking and skiing.

Weekends were the worst. On weekdays she could keep busy, pushing back the loneliness invasion, but not on Saturday and Sunday. On those days Mark kept the television going for hours, until the noise drove her to distraction. It was another good reason to retreat to the outdoors.

As the children entered their teens, they wanted less and less of her attention. They spent time alone in their rooms or with their friends. They had also inherited

Mark's love of electronics, with their endless collection of computerized gadgets.

As Joy pulled into the parking lot, she resolved to forget her concerns for a couple of hours. On the trail, she would admire the beautiful forests, hills, and blue sky.

She stepped out of the car, dropped her keys into her bag, hung it on her shoulder, and took a deep breath. It was a beautiful day, sunny with the cool crispness of spring. She looked around appreciatively as she headed toward the five-kilometre trail. This path wound through a stand of birches before reaching the denser foliage of the evergreens that had given the park its name.

As she rounded the first curve, she noticed a man standing under the shelter of a few birch trees on her left. He held his arms outstretched, palms upward, while four or five small brown birds perched on them and pecked at the seeds in his hands.

Joy stopped in surprise. She had never seen wild birds come near human beings, let alone perch on them. She stood quietly and watched for a few minutes, not wanting to frighten them away.

"How do you do that?" she asked in a tone barely above a whisper.

The man smiled. "I stay quiet, and the birds come to me. They know they can trust me," he replied in gently accented English.

Joy returned his smile. "Then I won't disturb you," she said as she continued her walk.

Next Friday evening, as Joy and Mark cleaned the kitchen, Joy hummed a happy tune.

"Are you going to the Moyers with me this evening?" she asked.

Mark frowned. "I'm too tired. Besides, I don't know those people. I wouldn't be comfortable with them."

"So I'll go by myself," replied Joy in a disappointed tone. This was the first time they had been invited to anyone's home in the four years they had lived in the city.

I'm going anyway, and I'll enjoy myself. It won't be the first time I've gone on a social outing without Mark.

Later, as she mingled with guests at the home of Jeff and Alma Moyer, her spirits rose. How ironic that Mark—friendly, talkative, likeable Mark—didn't care to meet new people while she—quiet, gentle Joy—welcomed the opportunity.

With a glass of punch in her hand and a plate of canapes on the coffee table in front of her, Joy sat on the couch and turned her attention to the conversation around her. She relaxed and chatted with the guests, nibbling on food and drinking punch.

She noticed a woman in a purple vest who had seated herself beside her.

"Why didn't your husband come?" the woman asked.

"He was tired," replied Joy. "He'd had a long day at work."

"Do you realize you're the only woman here who isn't coupled?"

Joy shrugged. "No, I hadn't. I don't pay attention to things like that." Who was this imperious creature? With an effort to be friendly, she offered, "I don't remember meeting you. My name is Joy."

"I'm Vanessa. You realize that most woman don't like an unattached woman at the party. They'll think she's out to steal their husbands."

Joy turned to face her. "If Jay and Alma don't want me here, they can ask me to leave—but otherwise I'm staying and enjoying the party."

She turned her back, and focused on the couple seated nearby.

The next day, Joy was still smarting from Vanessa's remarks. She tried to brush them off as ignorant snobbery, but the idea that she hadn't been welcome haunted her.

I don't belong with the married couples because Mark won't socialize with me, and I don't belong with the singles because I'm not single. So where do I belong?

She set out for Evergreen Park, leaving Mark watching a football game. She knew he would probably watch three games before the day was over.

At the park, she breathed deeply of the fresh air and started down the trail, happy to be outdoors. Around the first bend, she saw the man with the birds, in the same place he had stood a week ago.

Not wanting to frighten the birds, she stayed at a distance and waved.

"Hello," he greeted her quietly.

She watched for a few minutes as the birds finished pecking the last of the seeds. After they had flown away, she asked, "Do you come here often to feed the birds?"

"Yes, I do. It's relaxing to come out here, to get away from the stress of work."

"I feel the same way. There is too much noise and congestion in the city," she replied as they walked briskly down the path together. "This is the place I come to unwind."

"So, you must be a naturalist at heart."

"No, not really. I just enjoy being outdoors. I come here in the winter to ski with my daughter."

"Oh, you have a daughter?"

"Yes, my husband and I also have a son. And my name is Joy."

"I'm Anton," he replied. "I started my own business—in electronics. In my time off, this place refreshes me." His dark eyes sparkled as he pointed out various species of birds and plant life.

Joy felt refreshed as she listened to her companion talk. Anton obviously knew the wildlife and took pleasure in telling her the details of it.

At the end of the trail, Joy turned toward her car. "Thanks for your company."

She returned home in a cheerful frame of mind. She walked in the front door to find Mark and Erin folding laundry.

"Where's Nicholas?" she asked.

"He's at the soccer field. The coach called an extra practice." Erin picked up a pile of clothes and headed down the hall.

Mark continued to fold clothes. "Erin was after me to move, to go back to living near our families. She said she and Nicholas miss their cousins and grandparents."

Joy nodded, but said nothing. It was better to let Mark say what he had on his mind.

"You don't like living here either," he remarked in an accusing tone.

"No, I don't," she replied. "We have no friends here— no family either. Life is kind of dry without them. Visiting them once a year isn't often enough."

Joy wondered where this conversation was going; Mark hadn't talked to her this much since the last time he had changed jobs. He must have something in mind.

"Are you really thinking of moving?" she asked. "What about your job?"

"I can find another job. I want my family to be happy, and the children have never been really settled here." He paused, then stated proudly, "I can adjust anywhere."

"Let's discuss it some more. We would have to be ready to go during the summer." Joy realized that Mark had already made the decision, and she wasn't about to argue. Living nearer to her family, and having the chance to visit old friends, would make life more bearable. Perhaps it would cancel out the pain of Mark's neglect.

By next Saturday, Joy was more than ready to head for the hiking trails. The soccer coach had called for an extra practice, for which Nicholas was unhappy. "Does he think we're preparing for the Olympics?" he grumbled. "If we're still living here, I'm not going to play soccer next year. I have other things to do with my life."

As she drove into the parking lot at Evergreen Park, she saw Anton standing by his van. She smiled with pleasure; it would be good to walk and talk with him again.

"I was waiting for you," he said. "Shall we take the north trail? It's a little longer, but the view is worth it."

"The north trail will be fine."

As they headed for the trail, Anton asked, "Does your husband ever come hiking with you? I've never seen him here."

"No, he doesn't. He's not the outdoor type."

"What do you do together?"

Joy sighed. "Nothing, really. He reads and watches television. To be honest, I can't stand the constant blabbing of the television all day long. That's one of the reasons I go out so often—to escape the noise."

"That's too bad," he replied. "Don't you and your husband ever go out?"

Joy relished being with someone who was willing to listen. "About once a year, I guess. Two years ago, he took me to a banquet that his firm put on. I didn't think I'd like it. Formal dinners aren't my thing, but it turned out okay, and the people I met were fun and interesting. Another time he took the whole family to a bluegrass concert. It was a good evening. We all enjoyed it."

"So you prefer activities that are more casual."

"Yes, I do. But I'm willing to try new things." Joy sighed. "I wish Mark was willing to do that. Last summer, the children and I coaxed him to go to the lake for a picnic with us. He acted as if he was doing us a big favour. After we got there, he spent the whole time complaining about the flies and mosquitoes."

"He doesn't know what he's missing," said Anton quietly.

Joy suddenly became aware of how much she had said about herself and her husband—too much! She deliberately changed the subject. "What about you? What do you do when you aren't working or coming to the park?"

Anton smiled sadly. "Very little, really. Usually I meet people to promote my business. Coming to the park is my recreation."

"Mine, too. It's the only thing I do that isn't work."

They walked on in silence. As they approached the parking lot, Anton suggested, "Let's go for a cup of coffee."

Joy hesitated. *Go for coffee alone with a man—a married woman, a faithful married woman like me? But it's only coffee. What's the harm?*

Aloud she said, "Yes, I'd like that. I'll follow in my car."

"Okay," he said, unlocking his van.

Joy followed as he turned right outside the park entrance and headed south about half a mile. He then turned left at an intersection and pulled up not to a restaurant, but into the parking lot of an apartment block.

Okay, he's inviting me into his home—just him and me. I don't like this, but I suppose I have to go through with it.

She accompanied him into the building, up the elevator, and into his apartment.

Anton walked into the kitchen and grabbed the coffee pot.

"No coffee for me," Joy said. "I don't drink it. A glass of juice will be fine."

"I have grape juice. Will that be okay?"

"Yes."

He poured a glass of juice, handed it to her, and showed her into the living room. He sat down comfortably on the couch while Joy perched on the edge of a straight-backed chair.

They sat in silence while Joy drank her juice, then placed the glass on a nearby table. Where was their easy conversation of the hiking trail?

"You have a nice place here," Joy remarked, breaking the silence.

"Yes, it suits me."

Another minute or two of silence followed. Then Anton held out his arms and motioned with his hands. "Come here," he coaxed.

"No." Joy spoke plainly—no thank you, no explanation. She owed him nothing.

A minute later, she excused herself and left.

She drove around the corner to a side street where she parked by the curb. She couldn't go home yet; she needed time to think by herself.

What was I thinking? Is it even possible for a woman to have a male friend without sexual innuendo popping into it? Why couldn't my friend from Evergreen Park have been female? I don't want an affair. I don't want to break up my marriage. I don't want another man in my life. I just want more of the man I've already got!

Tears filled her eyes. Mark would never proposition a married woman—or a single woman either. Mark was planning to move and change jobs for the happiness of his children. Mark, in all the years they'd been married, had hardly ever said a critical word to her, had never begrudged her anything she wanted—except his companionship!

That's the hurt, she thought. *He doesn't willingly give me his time and attention.*

Joy parked for another twenty minutes, calming herself. Then she dried her tears, blew her nose, and drove home.

"You were gone a long time. I was about to come and look for you," Mark said as Joy entered the door. Then he noticed the traces of tears on her face. "What's wrong?"

Joy sat down wearily and shrugged.

"Please, tell me. I know that you're hurting. I want to know how I can fix things for you."

"I'm so lonely, it hurts."

"How can you be lonely? You have me and the children. You have the people at work and the people on the committee. You also have Ellen next door."

Joy didn't reply; Mark's response was no surprise. How could he understand? She resisted the urge to get up and walk away.

No, I won't walk away. This time I'm going to explain exactly what it's like, and what I want from him. He's going to understand if it takes hours. This time I'm not going to run away from a difficult discussion.

Joy turned to look squarely at her husband. "Mark, I would like to explain it to you. Will you listen without contradicting?"

He nodded. "I want my joyful Joy back. Tell me how I can help."

"First, I want you to know that I don't have any friends at work or on the environmental committee. They're just good co-workers, nothing more. I have made efforts, asking one or the other to meet me for coffee or lunch, but they are always too busy. What they really mean is that they aren't interested." She paused. "Do you understand that?"

"Okay. What about Ellen?" he asked. "Isn't she your friend?"

"No, she isn't. She smiles and chats a lot and acts friendly, but she only calls me when she wants me to drive her somewhere, or run an errand for her."

"So she's just using you."

"Right." Joy hesitated. How could she explain that the friendship she most wanted was with her husband? "Mark, the person I miss most is you."

"How can you say that?" he protested. "I always come home after work. I don't go to the bar with the other guys."

"Yes, I realize that." Joy spoke carefully. "But do you realize that when you are home, you don't spend time with me? You spend time with your mistresses!"

"Joy, that's not true! I have never chased other women, never wanted to. You know that!"

Joy stretched out her right arm and pointed her finger at the television. "I'm talking about that mistress." She placed her left hand on the stack of books and magazines. "And these mistresses. You know more about what's on the television and on the pages of your books than you know about your wife and children. Are we really so boring that you won't give us any of your attention? Are we really so dull and uninteresting?"

She brushed aside his attempt to interrupt, then spoke gently, "Mark, I'm not asking for much. I want about half an hour after work or after dinner, just for us to talk together. And would it be too much to ask you to take us out sometimes, even if it's only for a cup of coffee?"

"Is that all you want?" Mark asked in a puzzled tone. "It doesn't sound like very much."

"I don't want a lot, just a little of your undivided attention." With a mischievous smile, she added, "If coffee is too cheap for you, you can always take me out for a five-course dinner. The choice is yours, just like it was when we were dating."

Mark smiled tenderly. "To start with, suppose we go out to lunch tomorrow."

"Yes, I would like that."

"Do we have to go to a fast food place, just because the kids want to eat burgers and fries all the time?"

"No, we don't. We can go to a nice restaurant with table service. The children can order burgers if they want."

"Then it's a date." He picked up the remote control and clicked off the television. "Joyful Joy, I'm glad you told me this. Some women would say nothing. They would just run off with another man."

14.

A LAME HORSE AND A BRACELET

The pale sun of a late winter afternoon filtered through the curtains into the kitchen where two women sat at the table with coffee mugs. Kaitlin's red-blond hair fell to her shoulders, and her clear, fresh skin displayed her youth. Her eyes were clouded with sadness.

"Kaitlin, you haven't been yourself lately," her mother Jean said. "You have always been happy and upbeat, but something's changed. What happened? Why have you been down lately?"

"I'm tired of the way things are with me and Adam. I've been living here in his house, on his farm, with his equipment and livestock for three years. I want to get on with it. I want to get married and have babies."

"Have you told him that?"

"No, Mom. The man is supposed to ask the woman to marry him, not the other way around. Besides, men don't like to feel pressured."

"Oh, so it was okay for you to be pressured into his home and his bed, with no commitment, but when it comes to marriage, you're supposed to keep your mouth shut? Is that what you're saying?" her mother replied in a sarcastic tone.

"That's the way things are done."

"What you both need is some honest, straightforward communication. That's my opinion."

"I don't think I can do that," mumbled Kaitlin. She picked up the empty coffee mugs and carried them to the sink. She grabbed the flyer lying on the counter and waved it at her mother. "I left this advertisement for diamond rings where Adam could see it, hoping he would take the hint." She sighed. "What is he waiting for?"

Jean replied, clearly emphasizing each word. "Sweetie, men don't take hints. You have to talk to them directly and explain clearly what you want. I still say honest communication is the only way to go."

At that moment, they heard the sound of a motor in the yard and saw through the window a truck towing a horse trailer.

"Did Adam take the horses somewhere today?" asked Jean.

"Not that I know of."

She saw Adam Connor jump out of the truck and run into the house. He came into the kitchen and tossed a newspaper and two letters on the counter. They landed on top of the diamond ring flyer.

"Come and see what I've got for you," he said with a grin. "It's an early Christmas present."

Kaitlin and Jean grabbed their jackets and followed him outside.

Adam pointed to the brown mare inside the trailer. "I bought her from Glen Masters. She was his daughter's horse, but now that she's left home the mare needs someone to ride her. She's yours. Merry Christmas, honey."

"Oh, Adam, she's beautiful," Kaitlin exclaimed. She followed as Adam led the mare into the stable. Then she noticed the limp. "She's favouring her right leg."

Adam put the mare in the stall, removed the halter and lead, then bent down to examine her ankle and hoof. "I can't see what the problem is. If there's no change by tomorrow, I'll have the vet look at her." He straightened up. "Anyway, now you have a horse of your own. You've always said the other two horses were mine, not yours. This one's all yours."

"Thank you," said Kaitlin with a smile.

Dusk had fallen by the time they walked out of the stable. Kaitlin looked at the blazing sunset above the trim house, the well-maintained out-buildings, the stand of trees to the west, and sighed. It was a wonderful place, and a great life—but she was only a guest in it. She had kept it that way on purpose, of course; she had made no changes to the house or its furnishings. Her only possessions were her clothes and her car. If their arrangement failed, she could make an easy escape.

It hadn't failed; it just hadn't been completed. She was ready for marriage—in fact, had been ready ever since she had moved in. Was Adam ready? Would he ever be ready?

Adam put his arm around her shoulders. "Mom and Dad are expecting us for Christmas morning. They want us to stay for brunch. Is that okay with you?"

"Yes, that's fine. I told my mom we would come to their place in the afternoon, probably after three o'clock."

"One more thing, Kate. I have another gift for you, under the Christmas tree. I wanted you to have something you could unwrap."

"You've thought of everything," she replied.

Christmas morning arrived. Kaitlin busily packed two boxes of gifts, one for Adam's family and one for hers, and carried them out to the car.

Adam walked out of the barn where he had been feeding the stock. "I want to exercise the horses before I leave. Suppose you go to Mom and Dad's place in your car, and I'll come in the truck later."

"Okay, I'll do that. What about the mare? Is she any better?"

"No. The vet said she should rest her leg for a while yet."

"Okay, I understand," replied Kaitlin as she jumped into the car.

The Connor living room sparkled with Christmas in every corner. The delectable smell of bacon and sausages filled the house. With one accord, the family decided to eat their brunch first and then open gifts. Adam and Kaitlin, who had not eaten breakfast that morning, gladly ate their fill.

Gift-opening proved to be a lengthy activity, with each gift displayed to be admired by everyone. Adam's brother Dave, with his three-year-old Sam beside him, sat on the floor in front of the mound of presents and handed out each gift with great ceremony.

"Here's one for you, Kate, from Mom and Dad Connor," he said as he handed her a red and gold gift bag.

Mom and Dad Connor! They are not my in-laws, thought Kaitlin as she lifted a fluffy blue sweater out of the bag. She smiled as she turned to them. "Thank you. It's lovely."

The gift-opening lasted an hour and a half, much to the excitement of little Sam, who ran back and forth carrying gifts to his family members.

"This one's to Kaitlin from Adam," Dave said, picking up a tiny box. He feigned surprise. "I wonder what it could be! Here, Sam, take this to her quick. This is so exciting!"

Kaitlin's jaw dropped and her eyes sparkled as she took the small package from Sam.

Could it be? At last?

Conversation ceased. All eyes in the room turned toward her with anticipation.

She tore off the silver wrapping and opened the box. Her face fell with disappointment and her eyes filled with tears.

"What is it?" inquired Dave.

Kaitlin held up a glittering link bracelet to a chorus of awws and a few giggles. Anger and humiliation washed over her. She had always considered herself a patient girl, but this was too much. She jumped up from her chair and threw the rejected bracelet at Adam.

"Did you do this just to make me look like a fool?" she demanded. "Give a gift in a tiny little box that looks like it's going to be a ring—*the* ring?"

"But I gave you a horse," protested Adam in a puzzled tone.

Dave guffawed. "It was a lame horse, buddy."

"I'm too upset to stay here. I'm going home." Her tears flowing freely now, Kaitlin grabbed her jacket and headed for the door.

"I'll come, too," said Adam.

"No, you stay. I want to be by myself for a while. I've got to think this over."

Kaitlin drove home in tears, sobbing all the way. *It's time to make a change. I love Adam, but obviously he doesn't really love me. If he loved me, he would marry me. But I have to look out for myself. I have to go after what I want. I won't carry on feeling the way I do.*

At the house, she pulled her suitcases out of the closet, methodically filled them with her possessions, and carried them out to the door. Then she searched the desk for a blank sheet of paper, sat down at the kitchen table, and composed a letter.

Adam—I am through with playing house. I love you, but I want to get married and have babies. If I'm not going to get that from you, I am going to look for someone else. I am going to Mom and Dad's house. Make up your mind what you want, and let me know.

—Kaitlin

After leaving the letter on the kitchen table, she carried her luggage to the car and drove the five miles to her parents' home. There, she took refuge in the bedroom she used to share with her sister Rachel. She had to admit that in spite of her determination to follow up on her plans for marriage and children, the thought of Adam broke her heart. Her tears continued unabated for several hours while her parents, grandparents, brother, and sister ate their Christmas dinner in silent consternation.

Her mother came to the bedroom door with a message. "Adam phoned. He's coming to see you tomorrow morning. He thought he had better leave you alone for this evening." She added with a wry smile, "When I suggested communication, I didn't think of throwing a bracelet at him."

"I didn't plan on that either," replied Kaitlin. "I always thought of myself as an even-tempered person who didn't do things like that."

The next morning, the house was quiet with the lull that always follows a day of celebration. Kaitlin's tears had dried, her anger spent. Still firm in her resolve, though, she calmly reflected on her future.

The doorbell rang and Adam walked in without waiting for an answer. "We have to talk, Kaitlin. Will you come out to the truck?"

She put on her boots and jacket and followed him out the door.

Seated comfortably in the truck, Adam began, "Kate, if we're going to have any kind of future relationship, we need to be honest with each other—beginning now."

"I'm sorry I threw the bracelet at you," she said hesitantly. "In fact, I'm embarrassed that I acted in such a childish way."

"I'm not—if it settles matters between us. I didn't know you were so unhappy. I thought you liked living the way we were."

"I always figured that living together was a step toward marriage, but after three years I was tired of waiting for the next step. I want children, but I refuse to be a single parent. I want to have the same name as my children. I want to have everything settled for them."

"Why didn't you tell me this?"

"Because the man is supposed to propose marriage—and the woman is not supposed to pressure him."

"I see." Adam paused as he considered this information. "Then it's time to get on with it. Last night at home, all I could think about was what life would be like without you—how empty it would be. I don't want that."

He took her small hand in his large, sturdy one and looked into her eyes. "I love you, Kate, and I want you for life. I asked Glen to take back the mare, and he agreed. I'll get you another horse—a sound one you can ride right away. But most important—instead of a bracelet, how would you like a diamond ring?"

"Oh, Adam, do you really mean it?" exclaimed Kaitlin as tears sprang into her eyes. "You really want us to get married and have children? The answer is yes!"

Adam took her in his arms and held her close for a few minutes. Kaitlin sighed with contentment as she released herself and looked up at him.

"And let's keep the bracelet," she said. "After we're married, we'll hang it up somewhere in our home so we can both look at it, and when we disagree it will remind us to discuss the problem—and not throw things."

15.

A SPECIAL GIFT

THE NEIGHBOURHOOD WAS DECKED IN ITS CHRISTMAS finery on December 24. Assorted lights, garland, and figures sparkled in the joy of the season.

Louise, on her way home from helping with a party at the seniors' home, rang Martha's doorbell in the late afternoon. The elderly widow lived alone here, in one of the few houses undecorated, seemingly untouched by the warmth of the season. Martha had few visitors, for her ungracious manner repelled most people. Her children rarely visited. Not surprising, the neighbours said, in view of the poor reception they received.

Louise was the only one who wasn't dismayed by the old lady. Perhaps she recognized the hurt and loneliness behind her cool exterior. At any rate, she called frequently, even though she too often felt unwelcome.

"Hello, Martha. Isn't it a great day? It's wonderful to have such mild weather this December. It's so much easier to get out." Louise place her two bags, filled with hand-crafted decorations, on the kitchen table, and sat in the rocking chair that had once belonged to Martha's father.

"I suppose it is easier, but I wouldn't know. I don't go out much," replied Martha with a shrug. Her face was unsmiling as usual.

"Are you planning to stay home alone for Christmas?" asked Louise with concern. "You know we would still like you to spend the day with us."

"No, thank you. I don't celebrate Christmas. I had enough of it when the children were young. A lot of work and headache! And all they ever thought of was how many presents they were getting, and how expensive they were."

"But Christmas isn't about presents; it's about being together. Won't you reconsider? Our Christmas won't be very elaborate this year, since Richard was unemployed so long. He has a job now, but money is still tight."

"It's been a difficult year for your family, with finan-cial troubles and your mother's death. I hope you enjoy your day, but I would rather stay home."

Louise stood up and prepared to leave. As she picked up her bags, a paper chain fell out and lay on the floor, unnoticed for the present time. She paused at the door.

"The children have a gift for you," she said with a note of apology in her voice. "I hope you will accept it."

Martha's face softened. "Yes, I will accept it gracefully. I wouldn't disappoint your children."

As Louise continued her walk home, she thought of the past few months, filled with sorrow and uncertainty. Her mother had been a big part of her life, and her passing had left a void. Even so, she had died as she lived: at peace with herself.

Then Richard had been laid off, and uncertainty had fallen on the family. The three children, often selfish and demanding, surprised their parents. They accepted the reduced spending without complaint; they were sensitive to their father's feelings and tried to be helpful. Jonathan, aged fourteen, even offered the earnings from his paper route. Now, in the midst of frugal Christmas preparations, they searched for the ideal gift to bring a measure of joy to their lonely neighbour. Louise and Richard often thought it was worth the hardship to see their children in this new light.

That evening, Martha prepared and ate her supper. Then she relaxed in the living room where she watched a film version of Dickens' *A Christmas Carol*—her only observance of the season. The warmth of the story had always appealed to her, with the heart change in Scrooge.

After the film ended, she considered the drama she had just watched: Scrooge disliked Christmas because he was greedy; she disliked Christmas because she had been generous.

Every year Martha had shopped, baked, decorated, and attended Christmas concerts, all in preparation for a special celebration. Yet every year she had become a little more disillusioned with it all. Her children seemed to be concerned only with how much they were getting, with never a thought toward others, never an expression of appreciation to the mother who had prepared it all. It was as if it was their goal to acquire as many possessions as possible.

Remembering the simpler, more joyful Christmases of her childhood, Martha had tried to make changes. One year she had suggested that the family participate in Christmas dinner for the homeless. The children voiced unanimous objection, seeing only the ruin of their special day. Even her husband had remarked, "Why should you want to give our food to those people?" So much for that idea!

The next year she had started early on gifts, sewing and handcrafting special items. Her efforts were met with disappointment on Christmas morning. Aren't you going to buy us real stuff at the store? What are you trying to do, ruin Christmas? Her husband, in spite of his admiration for the attractive vest she had sewn for him, questioned the wisdom of making what could be more easily bought, telling her kindly that he didn't expect her to go to all that work. Tom was a good man and a good husband, but just a little short-sighted about such matters.

After that, the heart had gone out of her, not only for Christmas, but for other celebrations as well. If the family only valued expense, that's what they would receive. Why should she waste her time and energy on preparations that weren't appreciated? She shopped for gifts from the catalogue, avoiding the crowded malls. She bought Christmas treats, spending as little time cooking as possible. She simplified the decorating, much to the chagrin of the children. This time, Tom stood by her. If the children wanted more decorating, they must do it themselves; their mother did enough for them.

The years went by, the children grew up, Tom passed away, and the children established homes and families of their own. Often they invited their mother for Christmas. Usually she refused, dreading the elaborate celebration she found repeated in the next generation. It was peaceful in her home, even if it was lonely.

While Martha revisited Christmas past, Louise's children, in their home down the street, were wrapping their gifts.

"I'm so glad we found a special gift for Martha," remarked eight-year-old Sally.

———

Martha slept badly that night. She dreamed of Christmas. It whirled about her in the forms of the neighbourhood children revelling in their holiday pleasures. She was part of the dream herself, a caricature bound in paper chains, dancing grotesquely. One of the smiling children held out a gift to her. "You may accept the gift or accept the chains," he laughed.

In the morning, Martha arose from her disturbed sleep. She reflected on her dream as she prepared breakfast.

I suppose now I'm expected to change, and love Christmas, she thought with amusement as she carried her coffee cup to the old rocking chair and sat down. *Not a chance, not with a dream like that. It will take more than a dream.*

Martha spied a paper chain lying on the floor beside the chair. *What on earth is going on? Where did this come from?*

She gingerly picked up the chain and looked at it for a few seconds before dropping it. Her amazement was cut short by the sound of the doorbell.

Louise and her children entered, flushed with the excitement of Christmas.

"We have a present for you," announced Jonathan, handing Martha a colourfully wrapped parcel.

"It's a very special one," stated his small sister.

"A present! I hope you didn't go to much expense for it," said Martha with a twinge of conscience. She thought of Louise's careful ways during Richard's unemployment.

Peter was ready with an explanation. "It didn't cost us anything, but Mom says that sometimes the best gifts aren't the ones that cost the most money."

Martha nodded in agreement. She opened the attached card and read: *"To Martha, Merry Christmas, from Jonathan, Peter and Sally."*

Her curiosity aroused, Martha carefully unwrapped the package. Amid the colourful wrapping on her lap lay a book. Its black cover was worn and its pages frayed from repeated handling. She opened the front cover and read the name of the previous owner. The sacrificial nature of this well-used gift touched her.

Martha looked up at Louise. "But Louise, this was your mother's Bible! Surely you want to keep it for yourself as a memorial of her!"

"No, Martha. The children wanted to give you something special. We all discussed it and decided that we wanted you to have Mother's Bible. We thought it was the kind of gift you would like."

Tears filled Martha's eyes as a warmth she had not known in years flooded her heart. "Thank you, children. This is the best gift you could have given me." She opened her arms to embrace them. "And thank you, Louise. I've never said a kind word to you before, but I do appreciate all your thoughtfulness to your lonely neighbour."

"We're not just neighbours, we're friends," replied Louise. "That is, if you want to be."

"Yes, I do, and I'd like to accept your invitation to spend Christmas Day with you. You have the kind of Christmas I want—the kind I haven't known since I was a girl."

"Good! Then we'll see you later."

After Louise and the children left, Martha sat stroking the worn Bible. That family didn't give expensive gifts; they gave of themselves. She reflected that perhaps her dream had significance after all. She glanced at the foolish paper chain on the floor as her own chains of disillusionment fell silently away.